First Case
by

Kathi Daley

Acknowledgments

I want to thank the very talented Jessica Fischer for the cover art.

I so appreciate Bruce Curran, who is always ready and willing to answer my cyber questions, and Peggy Hyndman for helping sleuth out those pesky typos.

And, of course, thanks to the readers and bloggers in my life, who make doing what I do possible.

Thank you to Randy Ladenheim-Gil for the editing.

And finally I want to thank my sister Christy for always lending an ear and my husband Ken for allowing me time to write by taking care of everything else.

Books by Kathi Daley

Come for the murder, stay for the romance.

Zoe Donovan Cozy Mystery:
Halloween Hijinks
The Trouble With Turkeys
Christmas Crazy
Cupid's Curse
Big Bunny Bump-off
Beach Blanket Barbie
Maui Madness
Derby Divas
Haunted Hamlet
Turkeys, Tuxes, and Tabbies
Christmas Cozy
Alaskan Alliance
Matrimony Meltdown
Soul Surrender
Heavenly Honeymoon
Hopscotch Homicide
Ghostly Graveyard
Santa Sleuth
Shamrock Shenanigans
Kitten Kaboodle
Costume Catastrophe
Candy Cane Caper
Holiday Hangover
Easter Escapade
Camp Carter – *July 2017*

Zimmerman Academy The New Normal

Ashton Falls Cozy Cookbook

Tj Jensen Paradise Lake Mysteries by Henery Press
Pumpkins in Paradise
Snowmen in Paradise
Bikinis in Paradise
Christmas in Paradise
Puppies in Paradise
Halloween in Paradise
Treasure in Paradise
Fireworks in Paradise – *October 2017*

Whales and Tails Cozy Mystery:
Romeow and Juliet
The Mad Catter
Grimm's Furry Tail
Much Ado About Felines
Legend of Tabby Hollow
Cat of Christmas Past
A Tale of Two Tabbies
The Great Catsby
Count Catula
The Cat of Christmas Present
A Winter's Tail
The Taming of the Tabby – *May 2017*

Seacliff High Mystery:
The Secret
The Curse
The Relic
The Conspiracy
The Grudge

Sand and Sea Hawaiian Mystery:
Murder at Dolphin Bay
Murder at Sunrise Beach
Murder at the Witching Hour
Murder at Christmas
Murder at Turtle Cove
Murder at Water's Edge – *June 2017*

Road to Christmas Romance:
Road to Christmas Past

Writers' Retreat Southern Mystery:
First Case
Second Look – *July 2017*

The Writers:

Jillian (Jill) Hanford

Jillian is a dark-haired, dark-eyed, never-married thirty-eight-year-old newspaper reporter who moved to Gull Island after her much-older brother, Garrett Hanson, had a stroke and was no longer able to run the resort he'd inherited. Jillian had suffered a personal setback and needed a change in lifestyle, so she decided to run the resort as a writers' retreat while she waited for an opportunity to work her way back into her old life. Jillian shares her life with her partner in mystery solving, an ornery parrot with an uncanny ability to communicate named Blackbeard.

Jackson (Jack) Jones

Jack is a dark-haired, blue-eyed, never-married forty-two-year-old nationally acclaimed author of hard-core mysteries and thrillers, who is as famous for his good looks and boyish charm as he is for the stories he pens. Despite his success as a novelist, he'd always dreamed of writing for a newspaper, so he gave up his penthouse apartment and bought the failing *Gull Island News*. He lives in an oceanfront mansion he pays for with income from the novels he continues to write.

George Baxter

George is a sixty-eight-year-old writer of traditional whodunit mysteries. He'd been a friend of Garrett Hanson's since they were boys and spent many winters at the resort penning his novels. When he heard that the oceanfront resort was going to be used as a writers' retreat, he was one of the first to get on board. George is a distinguished-looking man with gray hair, dark green eyes, and a certain sense of old-fashioned style that many admire.

Clara Kline

Clara is a sixty-two-year-old, self-proclaimed psychic who writes fantasy and paranormal mysteries. She wears her long gray hair in a practical braid and favors long, peasant-type skirts and blouses. Clara decided to move to the retreat after she had a vision that she would find her soul mate living within its walls. So far the only soul mate she has stumbled on is a cat named Agatha, but it does seem that romance is in the air, so she may yet find the man she has envisioned.

Alex Cole

Alex is a twenty-eight-year-old, fun and flirty millennial who made his first million writing science fiction when he was just twenty-two. He's the lighthearted jokester of the group who uses his blond-haired, blue-eyed good looks to participate in serial dating. He has the means to live anywhere, but the thought of a writers' retreat seemed quaint and retro, so he decided to expand his base of experience and moved in.

Brit Baxter

Brit is George Baxter's twenty-six-year-old niece. A petite blond pixie, she decided to make the trip east with her uncle after quitting her job to pursue her dream of writing. She's an MIT graduate who decided her real love was writing.

Victoria Vance

Victoria is a thirty-seven-year-old romance author who lives the life she writes about in her steamy novels. She travels the world and does what she wants to who she wants without ever making an emotional connection. Her raven-black hair accentuates her pale skin and bright green eyes. She's the woman every man fantasizes about but none can ever conquer.

Townsfolk:

Deputy Rick Savage

Rick is not only the island's main source of law enforcement, he's a volunteer force unto himself. He cares about the island and its inhabitants and is willing to do what needs to be done to protect that which he loves. He's a single man in his thirties who seldom has time to date despite his devilish good looks, which most believe could land him any woman he wants.

Mayor Betty Sue Bell

Betty Sue is a homegrown Southern lady who owns a beauty parlor called Betty Boop's Beauty Salon. She can be flirty and sassy, but when her town or its citizens are in trouble, she turns into a barracuda. She has a Southern flare that will leave you laughing, but when there's a battle to fight she's the one you most want in your corner.

Gertie Newsome

Gertie Newsome is the owner of Gertie's on the Wharf. Southern born and bred, she believes in the magic of the South and the passion of its people. She shares her home with a ghost named Mortie who has been a regular part of her life for over thirty years. She's friendly, gregarious, and outspoken, unafraid to take on anyone or anything she needs to protect those she loves.

Meg Collins

Meg is a sixty-six-year-old volunteer at the island museum and the organizer of the turtle rescue squad. Some feel the island and its wildlife are her life, but Meg has a soft spot for island residents like Jill and the writers who live with her.

Barbara Jean Freeman

Barbara is an outspoken woman with a tendency toward big hair and loud colors. She's the friendly sort, with a propensity for gossip who owns a bike shop in town.

Sully

Sully is a popular islander who owns the local bar.

The Victims and Suspects:

Rayleen Oswald
Victim #1—Went to Waverly Island with high school sweetheart Troy Wheeler. Trevor Bailey introduced the couple.

Trevor Bailey
Victim #2—Went sailing with his girlfriend, Brooklyn Vanderbilt, his best friend, Jason Rogers, and Jason's girlfriend, Carrie Quincy.

Joshua Vanderbilt
Victim #3—Went sailing with his cousin, Brooklyn Vanderbilt.

Troy Wheeler
Still lives on the island; a bank manager and town council member who went on the sailing trip with Rayleen Oswald, who he argued with prior to her death.

Brooklyn Vanderbilt
Still lives on the island; a third-grade teacher married to Flip Johnson, who was not on the trip. They have two children.

Jason Rogers
Still lives on the island, doing seasonal jobs. Eleven years ago his father owned the boat on which the group set sail. He invited his girlfriend, Carrie, his best friend, Trevor, and Trevor's girlfriend, Brooklyn, to go sailing when a storm rolled in, stranding them on a deserted island.

Carrie Quincy
Still lives on the island and works at Gertie's. She went sailing with her boyfriend, Jason Rogers.

Katrina Pomeroy

Current victim who moved away after the Massacre eleven years ago but returned to the island on the eleventh anniversary of the event. She owned an art gallery in Charleston, South Carolina.

Chapter 1

Saturday, October 14

The fact that Katrina Pomeroy had been murdered was in and of itself a newsworthy event. The fact that she had been murdered on Friday, October 13, exactly eleven years after she'd been one of five teenagers to survive the Friday the Thirteenth Massacre, made her passing worthy of notice by the national news agencies I used to work for. When an old editor of mine offered me the chance to write a human-interest piece about Katrina's life and subsequent death, I jumped at the chance. An article such as this had all the makings of becoming the exposé I, Jillian Hanford, needed to relaunch my presently defunct career. Of course to make the sort of impact I was after, I'd not only need to write about Katrina's unusual life, but to answer the question of who was responsible for her death.

I knew I'd need help to accomplish my goal, so I gathered my friends on a dark and stormy night and, with the help of fellow writer George Baxter, presented a proposal.

"Rayleen Oswald was the first to die," George shared in a raspy voice as thunder rumbled in the distance. "She was stabbed thirteen times and then propped against a tree that, eerily enough, would be struck by lightning before the horrific night had come to an end."

A flash of light pierced the sky, causing everyone gathered in the three-story home we shared to gasp as they waited for the clap of thunder we knew would follow. The house, which was part of the rundown resort I had agreed to manage temporarily, shook as the wind battered the island from the south, causing the tension in the room to intensify.

George continued. "Most felt that, as the first victim, Rayleen was the killer's intended target, the others who died merely victims of circumstance. I'm not sure we can ever know what was in the killer's mind and heart, but despite the killer's motive, or lack thereof, two more died before the sun rose in the morning sky."

Rain streamed down the windows, creating a feeling of isolation in the room that was illuminated by only the light from the fire and a few flickering candles we'd set around to offset the inky darkness created when the electricity had flickered and then gone out. It wasn't uncommon for strong storms to batter the small islands off the South Carolina coast, but I was new to the area and had yet to develop the backbone necessary to easily weather such storms.

"Why were the kids on the island in the first place?" Clara Kline, a sixty-two-year-old, self-proclaimed psychic and paranormal mystery writer, asked her traditional mystery counterpart.

George took a puff from his pipe before he spoke again. "The day had started off sunny and mild. A group of teens from the local high school decided to cut class and go sailing, even though the local weather service predicted that a major storm would blow in by midafternoon. Now, the kids, having grown up on the island, were familiar with local weather patterns, and most were excellent sailors, but for reasons that have never been fully understood, they failed to return to the marina before the tropical storm rolled in. When the teens realized they weren't going to make it back to Gull Island, they decided to take shelter in one of the abandoned structures on Waverly Island."

"Waverly Island?" asked Brit Baxter, George's twenty-six-year-old niece and the newest member of our group.

"It's about fifteen miles north of us," I answered in George's stead.

Brit was not only new to the group but new to the writers' retreat and Gull Island, so I wasn't surprised she was unfamiliar with the small settlement on the nearby island that had been occupied a half century ago but had been destroyed by a hurricane and never rebuilt. I glanced at Blackbeard, the outspoken parrot I'd inherited when I took over as manager of the resort my half brother, Garrett Hanford, owned. It appeared he was listening intently to the story, which sort of creeped me out; he was, after all, a bird. Blackbeard nodded in my direction, which made me flinch. It had occurred to me on more than one occasion that the assertion by Clara that the large tropical transplant was really an apparition in disguise might not be as wild a claim as I'd originally believed.

"So eight teenagers took refuge on a deserted island in the middle of a tropical storm..." Alex Cole, a fun, flirty millennial who'd made his first million writing science fiction when he was just twenty-two trailed off, thereby encouraging George to go on.

"The shelter where the teens sought refuge was within the walls of a structure that had been destroyed more than thirty years before. They built a fire for warmth and decided to wait out the storm. At some point after they settled in, Rayleen and her boyfriend, Troy, got into a fight. Rayleen stormed off, and the next time anyone saw her, she had been stabbed thirteen times and left leaning against a tree that had just been struck by lightning. The specifics of this story are complex," George warned. "I'm going to suggest we keep to the overview this evening and then examine the bones of the mystery at a later time."

"Sounds fine by me," Brit answered. "But I still want to hear the end of the story."

"Very well." Charles refilled his glass of brandy from the bottle on the table. "After Rayleen was found, the others feared they weren't alone on the island. So, after much discussion, they did what the characters in any horror movie do: They split up to take a look around. After an exhaustive search in the pouring rain, with gale-force winds hampering their every step, the seven remaining teens finally concluded that if there had been someone else on the island they were long gone. They returned to the structure where they'd initially set up camp and waited for the storm to pass."

"And then? You said there were three victims," Alex pointed out.

"Why is it that young people today are so anxious to get to the finish line? Stories such as this one should be drawn out and savored."

Alex gave Charles an impatient look.

"Anyway," Charles continued, "after a long day battling both the storm and their fear, everyone began to drift off to sleep. No one claimed to know exactly when the second victim, Trevor Bailey, left the others, but at some point his girlfriend, Brooklyn Vanderbilt, woke up and noticed him missing. When he didn't return after almost a half hour, Brooklyn went looking for him. She found him impaled on an old ship's anchor."

The room fell silent as Charles paused for everyone to digest what he'd said. The shadows created by the wood fire in the old stone fireplace lent an eerie feeling to the already spooky aura that had been created by the storm and the story. Alex got up and poured himself a tall glass of whiskey while Brit wrapped her arms around her legs, as if attempting to make herself as small as possible. I wondered what must have gone through the minds of the teens that night. Knowing you were trapped on an island with a homicidal maniac had to be the most horrifying thing one could imagine. A representative from the sheriff's office had interviewed the survivors, but they'd been so traumatized that their memories had been distorted. In the end, the stories each told were so completely different as to be rendered useless.

"And the third victim?" Alex finally asked. Most of the time you could count on Alex to interject a bit of humor into a tense situation, but tonight, as the storm raged outside and Charles shared this very true story, he looked as spooked as anyone.

"The third victim was a boy named Joshua Vanderbilt. He was Brooklyn's cousin, who was visiting Gull Island. Joshua was found facedown in a freshwater pond. Some said he'd passed out due to the large quantity of alcohol he'd consumed that day and his death by drowning was an accident; others insisted he was murdered."

"So Brooklyn was connected to two of the victims," Alex commented. "She was the girlfriend of victim number two, Trevor Bailey, and the cousin of victim number three, Joshua

Vanderbilt. Was she related in any way to victim number one, Rayleen Oswald?"

"Trevor was friends with Rayleen," I answered. "In fact, it was Trevor who introduced Troy and Rayleen to each other. As far as I can tell from my preliminary research, a lot of people have spent a significant amount of time looking at both stated and secret relationships between the kids who set off on the boat that day. The reality is, this is a small island, and except for Joshua, the teens all went to the same school, so they were all connected to one another in some way."

By this point everyone in the room was frowning. Not that I blamed them; the story was not only tragic but confusing as well. Finally Clara asked about the names of the other survivors and where they currently lived, if known.

"Brooklyn Vanderbilt still lives on the island," George provided. "She teaches third grade at Gull Island Elementary School. She's married to a local contractor, Flip Johnson. They have two children, a boy and a girl. She's a well-respected and liked member of the community."

"So theoretically Brooklyn would be available to be interviewed," Brit commented.

"Theoretically," George answered. "Another survivor, Carrie Quincy, also still lives on the island. She works as a waitress at Gertie's. I'm sure most of you have met her."

"Carrie from the diner was on the island that night?" Alex asked.

"She was, although she prefers not to speak about what happened. She was with her boyfriend at the time, Jason Rogers."

"And Katrina Pomeroy?" Brit asked.

"She left the island after the incident. Prior to her death, she owned an art gallery in Charleston."

"I heard her body was found at the foot of the old pier," Alex commented. "It seems as if she'd been pushed. Do you think her murder is related to the Friday the Thirteenth Massacre?"

"Perhaps," I answered.

"So if she'd moved to Charleston, what was she doing here when she was killed?"

"That's one of the unanswered questions I've been pondering," I said.

In the past twenty-four hours I'd been struggling unsuccessfully to outline a news article about Katrina's murder. I'd finally brought my problem to Charles, who, after quite a bit of discourse, had suggested we bring the puzzle to the rest of the writers' group.

"Who owned the boat the kids sailed on?" Clara asked.

"Jason Rogers. He still lives on Gull Island. He's a marine mechanic and works over at the marina in the summer. During the off-season he does odd jobs for Troy Wheeler, who, as you'll remember, was Rayleen's boyfriend at the time of her death. Troy works as a bank manager. He also serves on the island council."

The group fell into silence, trying to process everything that had been said. Although we all were writers, each of us had our own niche and tended to work alone. The writers' group had begun meeting a couple of times a week to discuss our work the previous summer, when Charles was researching a true crime for his latest whodunit. He'd hit a roadblock and asked Clara, Alex, and me for help. The result of our work was a bestseller for Charles and a clue that led the Charleston PD to a real-life killer.

From that point we decided to use one another as a sounding board when we ran into snags in our projects. Brit had just moved out to the resort the previous week, after deciding that her degree in business was getting her nowhere. After a bit of introspection she'd realized she wasn't taking the business world by storm because her real love was writing. Because she was Charles's niece there was no question that she'd be admitted into the group even though she had yet to solve her first mystery or publish her first book.

"When's your article due?" Brit asked.

"They want it by the end of next week. I could turn it in minus a resolution to the murder, but I'd really like to solve the mystery before we go to print. I could use everyone's help."

"I'm in," Brit answered. "Just let me know what you need me to do."

"I'll help as well," Clara offered.

"I think that even if the entire group commits we're going to have an uphill battle, though I'm up for the challenge," Alex agreed. "When's Victoria going to be back? I'm not sure we can do this without her snarky comments to keep us on track."

Victoria Vance, a best-selling novelist who specializes in steamy romances, is my best friend.

"Not until Monday. The convention is over tomorrow morning, but she planned to visit friends and do some shopping before heading home."

"Have you spoken to Deputy Savage?" Alex asked. "I'm sure he's the one investigating Katrina Pomeroy's murder. He must have established a list of suspects by now."

"I called to speak to him, but he isn't sharing. I guess I don't blame him. My interest in the case is journalistic, while his is in bringing the person responsible for killing Katrina to justice. I guess I'll need to pay him a visit in person, where my powers of persuasion can shine through."

"Couldn't hurt to have a cop's perspective," Alex commented.

"What *do* you know about Katrina and her death?" Clara wondered.

"That shortly after the five survivors of the Friday the Thirteenth Massacre were rescued, Katrina's family left the island. She pretty much dropped off the radar, though I found an article that said she was living in Charleston, where she owned an art gallery. It seems she was doing quite well. I have no idea why she happened to be on Gull Island exactly eleven years after the horrific night that sent her running in the first place. If she was as traumatized as the article made it sound it makes no sense that she'd return to the island, especially on the anniversary."

"Have you spoken to the other survivors?" Alex asked.

"Not yet. I just got the call from my old editor this morning, and with the storm, I haven't had a chance to work on it other than to do some computer research and discuss the matter with Charles. It isn't going to be an easy mystery to solve, but I feel if anyone can get to the bottom of the whole thing we can."

"I think we have as good a shot as anyone," Charles agreed.

"My sense is that we'll find our way to an answer, but I'm exhausted. I think I'll head upstairs," Clara announced.

Alex and Brit agreed they could use some shut-eye as well, so they followed Clara up the stairs to the second floor, where most of the house's ten bedrooms were located.

"What do you really think?" I asked Charles when the three of them had gone. Although I'd only met him a few months ago, I felt I could trust and depend on him more than anyone else in my life. Maybe it was the kindness in his faded blue eyes, the nostalgia of the worn tweed jackets he favored, the smell of tobacco coming from his cherrywood pipe, or the careful way he considered every situation, but from the moment I met him I'd felt like I'd finally been united with the grandfather I'd always longed for but never known.

"I think this is going to turn out to be a difficult and complicated case. The initial murders occurred over a decade ago and for one reason or another have never been solved. The death of Katrina Pomeroy appears to have occurred in isolation, with no witnesses."

"So you think I should drop it?" I tucked a lock of my long brown hair behind my ear to keep it from falling across my face.

"Not necessarily. If the case had been easy to solve it would have happened already and would therefore be of little interest to your editor or us. We have captured Alex's interest, which is a good thing. The kid is young and cocky and occasionally tests my last nerve, but he is also bright, creative, and industrious. He has a unique way of weeding through facts and honing in on the root of the matter. I have a feeling if we can channel his focus he will turn out to be a huge asset."

"And the others?"

"I love Brit. She is my very favorite niece. But she is young and untested. She still needs to grow into her place with the group. I'm not sure she will be a lot of help with this case, but given time, I'm sure she will fit in. As for Clara, we both know she has the potential to provide the precise insight that can make the difference between success and failure. I think the fact that teens were involved in this case has caused her to take a step back emotionally. It is my sense, however, that in the end she will make the connection to provide the insight we need."

Clara wrote paranormal mysteries and claimed to have psychic powers. Her books were wonderful, but I hadn't decided if the psychic part was true. Clara had provided a key insight that had allowed us to solve the case Charles had been working on the previous summer, but she tended to become emotionally involved in whatever case we were discussing, which seemed to block her ability to get a clear and concise reading. There was a part of me—the long-suppressed child part—that really wanted to believe in her psychic powers, but I was no longer a child, and the pragmatist in me had pretty much decided Clara was just very observant and that was why she picked up on subtle clues others missed.

"The reality is," Charles added, "we have nothing to lose by attempting to figure this out. If we do you will have a wonderful twist for your article and a killer will have been brought to justice; if we don't, we will only have wasted a few hours of our lives."

"Thanks, Charles. I only have a week to turn in my article, so I plan to give it my all. I'm not sure if the case is solvable, but I'd like to give it a try." I could hear thunder rumbling in the distance. "It looks like we're in for the second wave of rain the forecasters said was coming."

"I think I will go up and get settled in before it gets here."

"Me too. I'll see you in the morning."

I tossed another log on the fire before heading upstairs. Normally Blackbeard slept in a cage in the library, but tonight, with the storm and all, I'd decided to bring him upstairs and have him sleep in my room at the top of the house. One of the first things I'd done upon moving in was remodel the attic and turn it into a bedroom. Not only did the third story have the best view in the house, but being alone on my own floor afforded me a certain degree of privacy.

"What about you?" I asked the bird as I carried him up the two flights of stairs. "Do you think we have a chance of solving this complicated case?"

"Captain Jack, Captain Jack."

I smiled at my brighter-than-average bird. Leave it to him to come up with the exact person I'd need to bring this story home.

Bring the story home. God, how I missed that.

Chapter 2

Sunday, October 15

Jackson Jones isn't your typical newspaperman. As a multiple *New York Times* best-selling author, it would seem he held the world in his hands, but Jackson had a dream. His grandfather had owned a chain of small newspapers on the West Coast when he was growing up. From the time he was a toddler, Jack would sit and watch the printing press spit out the daily news. Jack knew that someday he wanted to work for a newspaper, but his dreams had been put on hold after he sold over two million copies of a novel he'd written on a whim when he was just nineteen.

When the book reached best-seller lists around the world, Jackson Jones, with his exceptional good looks and charm, had become an overnight sensation. Over the course of the next twenty-three years he wrote twenty-three more best-selling novels. A year before, he'd realized he was getting restless despite his success. When he learned the fledging *Gull Island News* was for sale, he'd bought it, sold his penthouse apartment, and moved to Gull Island to follow his dream. The newspaper lost money on every edition it printed, but Jackson didn't care about the money; he continued to make more than enough to live on from his novel sales.

I met Jack shortly after moving to Gull Island and we'd become instant friends.

"I was hoping you'd stop by," Jack greeted me as I walked in the front door of the newspaper office.

I tossed my backpack on the front counter. "I guess you heard about Katrina Pomeroy."

"Yes. Are you writing a story?"

"I am. I assume you are as well."

"You assume correctly."

I grabbed a piece of hard candy from the dish Jack kept for his customers. "My piece is a human-interest thing, detailing the connections between the deaths of Rayleen Oswald, Trevor Bailey, and Joshua Vanderbilt eleven years ago and Katrina Pomeroy's two days ago. I have until the end of the week to turn it in, so I thought I'd do some digging to see if I can find something more than the obvious. I'm sure you already have a story to run in tomorrow's paper, but I was wondering if you'd like to work with me on a follow-up piece."

"I take it you have a jumping-off point?"

I nodded. "I also have Charles, who was around when the first murders occurred, and he's willing to help. You in?"

"I'm in."

"Perfect. The gang and I are meeting at the house tonight to come up with a strategy. Say around six? I'll make dinner."

"Six is great. I'll see you then. And Jill, if you decide to get a head start on the snooping, be careful. Four people have already died; I'd hate to have it be five."

"I'll be careful," I promised as I walked out, even though what I really wanted to do was remind him that I'd been an investigative reporter for a major newspaper for almost twenty years and had put myself in more danger then than I was likely to find on Gull Island.

I headed over to Gertie's on the Wharf for coffee and conversation. Now that the storm had passed the town was filled with residents out in the street and on the sidewalks helping to clean up. It was amazing how much damage a little wind and rain could do, although I guess if I were perfectly accurate the storm we'd experienced had amounted to more than a little wind and rain.

Gertie was one of the first people I'd met when I'd arrived on the island, and she remained one of my favorite. She was a friendly, outspoken, gregarious individual with a childlike ability to suspend disbelief that I secretly longed to emulate.

"Morning, Gertie," I called to the plump woman behind the counter.

"Mornin', sugar. Mortie said you'd be by."

Mortie was the ghost Gertie claimed had lived in her house for the past thirty years.

"Did he tell you what I'd want?"

"Said you'd be askin' about those kids who died a while back."

The fact that I was not only an ex-reporter but a huge snoop should have alerted Gertie to the reason for my visit even without a heads-up from Mortie, but I enjoyed the fantasy Gertie perpetuated and usually went with it.

"And does Mortie know anything about those kids that might be helpful?"

"You writin' a story?"

"I am."

"Mortie has information to share, but you know he doesn't want his name used as a source."

I suppressed a grin. "I promise to leave his name out of it. So what does he know?"

Gertie poured me a cup of coffee and settled in across the counter from me. There was only one other table occupied in the restaurant and the couple there already had their food, so it looked as if Gertie would have a few minutes to chat. In my dealings with her I'd learned that not only was Mortie a surprisingly reliable source but Gertie, who doubled as café owner and town gossip, usually had more than her share of comments to add.

"Mortie had a chat with the girl who fell to her death the other day and she shared with him that she wasn't pushed, as most people assume."

I wasn't expecting that. "What do you mean, she wasn't pushed? They found her body on the rocks at the foot of the pier. Did she fall?"

"That girl wasn't pushed and she didn't fall; she jumped."

"Jumped? She committed suicide? Why?" When I'd first heard they'd found Katrina's body I'd assumed she'd either fallen or been pushed. Given the coincidence that she'd died exactly eleven years after her friends had been murdered, it was logical to assume she'd been murdered.

Gertie shrugged. "Mortie doesn't know, but if you ask me, someone strugglin' with a guilty conscious might be motivated to end the torment."

There was no possible way that either Gertie or Mortie could know whether Katrina was pushed or jumped, but the theory that Katrina's death might not have been a murder after all seemed worth considering.

"I take it you're insinuating Katrina had a guilty conscious because she was the one who killed her friends eleven years ago."

"That's exactly what I'm sayin'."

"Why? Why would she do such a thing in the first place?"

"Why does anyone ever kill anyone? Unrequited love, jealousy, unresolved anger, money?"

I stopped to think about what Gertie was saying. Based on what I'd heard, Katrina had been invited on the sailing trip by Carrie Quincy, who'd been Jason Roger's girlfriend. It was Jason's boat the kids had taken out that day and, again according to what I'd heard, Jason initially invited only Carrie, his best friend Trevor, and Trevor's girlfriend, Brooklyn. I assumed Brooklyn was the one who'd invited her cousin Joshua, but I wasn't sure how the other three kids ended up on the boat. At the time of the murders, the police had suspected Rayleen was the intended victim and Trevor and Joshua had been in the wrong place at the wrong time. If Katrina was the killer that meant her motive would have had something to do with Rayleen.

"Do you know how Katrina and Rayleen were connected?" I asked Gertie. "Were they friends? Enemies?"

"I'm not sure, but Carrie would know. She was friends with Katrina in high school."

"Will she be in today?"

"No. I gave her some time off. She was pretty upset when she heard about Katrina. Poor thing. She hadn't seen her old friend in years, but she still took it hard."

"Can you give me Carrie's phone number? I'd like to speak to her if she's up to it."

"I'm not sure she'll want to talk about it just yet. I'll call her to see how she feels about it. If she's willin' to speak to you I'll text you her address."

"That sounds fair. And thanks, Gertie. You're always so helpful."

"Don't thank me; thank Mortie."

"I will. The next time I see him." Which would be never because he was a ghost.

Outside Gertie's I paused, considering what to do next. What I really wanted to do was head over to the sheriff's office to have a chat with Deputy Rick Savage. I assumed he was in his midthirties and he was a lifelong Gull Island resident, so chances were he was already working in local law enforcement at the time of the Massacre. I'd bumped into Savage a time or two in the past and he'd made it very clear he didn't welcome questions or interference from reporters—or anyone else, for that matter—who came around asking questions about an active investigation. Still, I hadn't become a top investigative reporter by caring who was disposed to talk to me, so I got back in my car and headed across town to the sheriff's office.

"I was afraid you wouldn't take no for an answer after your call and would be by today," Deputy Savage said sourly when I arrived.

"It's good to see you again too. I heard your softball team won the interisland tournament. Congratulations."

He frowned. "What do you want? I'm sure your visit today wasn't to congratulate me."

"Actually, you're correct. I *am* honing my ability to engage in small talk, but the real reason I'm here is to substantiate a tip I received that Katrina Pomeroy jumped from Thompson's Pier rather than being pushed."

I watched Deputy Savage's face as he quickly masked both his confirmation and his surprise.

Gotcha.

"I can see by your reaction that my source was correct. Would you care to comment on the fact that Katrina apparently committed suicide?"

"I wouldn't care to comment on anything regarding this case. Who exactly told you that Katrina jumped?"

"My source wishes to remain anonymous. Is it your opinion that Katrina committed suicide as a reaction to feelings of guilt? Might we have finally solved the three murders that took place on that October 13 eleven years ago?"

"I didn't confirm or deny that Katrina jumped from the pier," Deputy Savage reminded me.

I winked. "Sure you did."

I could see Savage was becoming frustrated by my questions. I did live on the island and I wanted to enjoy a peaceful existence, so the last thing I wanted to do was make this small-town cop angry.

I backed off just a bit in the interest of harmony. "Look, I know I can be pushy. I built a reputation on being pushy. And I'll admit I'm working on a story. But I really don't want to make any waves. You know that once the story gets out that one of the survivors of the Friday the Thirteenth Massacre has become a recent Friday the Thirteenth victim there are going to be other reporters nosing around. I've already spoken to Jackson Jones, and in the interest of continued harmonious relations, we've agreed to work together. He's after a newsy piece for the local paper and I'm after an exposé for a national magazine, so we aren't in competition anyway.

What I'm going to suggest is that you join the team and work with Jack and me."

Deputy Savage frowned but didn't answer.

"You know we're going to dig around with or without your help and cooperation. Wouldn't you rather be on the inside so you can keep an eye on us?"

Savage looked at me with a look of disgust and amazement on his face. "You really are something."

"Thank you." I knew he didn't mean that in a complimentary way, but it served my purpose to let it go. "So do we have a deal? Are we going to work together?"

"What exactly do you mean by *work together*?"

"If we find a clue or uncover an important piece of information, we'll fill you in, and if you find a clue or uncover an important piece of information, you fill us in."

Deputy Savage still didn't answer, but I could see he was considering my proposal.

"If we were in a big city your boss would be holding a press conference to fill reporters in on the specifics. All I'm asking is that we accomplish the sharing of information on a one-on-one basis considering a press conference isn't likely to happen on the island." I waited for a couple of beats before continuing. "If you don't keep us in the loop, Jack and I are going to be forced to go off on whatever tangents present themselves. Inadvertently reporting the wrong news could have an adverse effect on the search for the truth, even if that news was reported in good conscious."

"Are you trying to blackmail me?"

"What?" I was certain my face reflected the appropriate degree of outrage. "I can assure you that my intention isn't to blackmail but simply to point out the advantage of a partnership."

"So if I say no you aren't going to print theories based on rumors and hearsay?"

"I didn't say that. If rumors and hearsay are all I have, then rumors and hearsay will be what I print, but I can assure you that *blackmail* isn't a word I would use to describe what I'm proposing." I took a deep breath before continuing. "As I said before, I don't want to make waves if I don't have to. In fact, I'd like for us to be friends. This is a small island and we're both part of a very close-knit community. I promise to be sensitive to the job you're faced with and will take the fact that you're dealing with an ongoing investigation into account before I publish anything. I can't speak for Jack, but my sense is that he'll agree to the same. So how about it? Do we cooperate?"

Savage crossed his arms over his chest in a defensive posture but finally agreed. "What do you want to know?"

"Did Katrina Pomeroy jump to her death?"

"I don't know. There were no eyewitnesses that I know of, but she didn't appear to have any defensive wounds and her injuries are congruent with those of someone who had jumped."

Dang; I had to hand it to Gertie's ghost. The guy really did seem to know what was going on in the world of the recently dead and dearly departed.

Chapter 3

After I left the sheriff's office I headed toward the address Gertie had texted me. She'd spoken to Carrie, who was willing to share what she knew with me, provided that, like Mortie, I kept her name out of any article I wrote. As I drove toward the southernmost end of the island, where Carrie lived, I schooled myself to bring out my sensitive side, to show compassion for a woman who had suffered so much loss in her life.

"Carrie Quincy, I'm Jillian Hanford."

"I know who you are," Carrie informed me without opening the screen door she was standing behind. "Gertie said you wanted to talk to me."

"I do. Would you mind if I came in for a few minutes?"

She hesitated.

"I promise not to name you as the source of anything you tell me. Gertie said you'd like to remain anonymous."

She unlatched the door. "Gertie said I could trust you and I trust her, so I guess it's okay."

I looked at Carrie with sincere compassion. "I really do understand how difficult this must be for you. What you went through is something no one should ever have to experience. I promise I'll make our interview as painless as possible."

"Come into the living room. We can talk there."

I followed her down the hall and took a seat on the sofa as she indicated. I sensed she wouldn't be at all open to our conversation being taped, so I asked if it would be all right if I took notes. The timid woman nodded her consent.

I took out my notebook and turned to a blank page before I began. "I actually have questions about two related but separate incidents: Katrina Pomeroy's presence on the island as well as her death two days ago, and the events surrounding the deaths of Rayleen Oswald, Trevor Bailey, and Joshua Vanderbilt eleven years ago. Are you okay speaking about both?"

She nodded. I hoped she'd be comfortable enough to actually speak at some point.

"Let's start with Katrina," I suggested. "I understand that prior to the incident eleven years ago you and she were friends."

"Yes. In a way. Katrina didn't have a lot of close friends, but we shared a couple of classes and talked from time to time."

"Can you tell me how the two of you both happened to be with the group who went sailing on the day of the murders?"

Carrie appeared to be nervous. She squirmed around in her seat as she attempted a reply. "We, Katrina and me, were supposed to be in school that day. I had been dating Jason Rogers for a few weeks, and I was really in to him. When he asked me to go sailing I jumped at the chance. Initially there were just supposed to be the two couples going: Jason and me and Jason's best friend, Trevor, and his girlfriend, Brooklyn. I think the guys had romance on their minds."

"Yes, it would seem. So how did the others come to go along?"

She fidgeted with the hem of her shorts as she continued. "Brooklyn's cousin Joshua was in town. I guess she told Trevor that she wouldn't be able to go unless he came along; her dad was depending on her to keep him occupied. I really wanted to go, so when I found out about Joshua I decided to invite Katrina to even things out."

"And the others? Rayleen Oswald and Troy Wheeler?"

"I'm not sure who invited them. They just showed up at the boat. I know Trevor and Rayleen were friends, so maybe when he realized it wasn't going to be just the two couples he invited her to go along."

"What happened after everyone arrived at the marina?"

"Jason and the guys got the sails up and we headed out to sea. Someone had brought beer, so everyone started drinking. It was a warm, sunny day and it seemed like everyone was in a good mood. We were all having a lot of fun when the storm blew in. Jason said we needed to head back, so he turned the boat around and headed toward home. After we'd been sailing for a while the wind got really bad and Jason said we weren't going to make it. He said he knew of an island that was closer than Gull, so he headed in that direction instead."

"And then?"

"And then it started to rain. We managed to get to shore before the thunder and lightning started, but I could tell we were in for a really bad storm. I was scared. We all were."

So far Carrie's story paralleled what I'd already learned. "What happened after you landed on the island?"

"There was a settlement there years ago, before it was destroyed in a storm. All the people had moved away, but there were still some buildings. Or at least parts of buildings. We picked the one that looked the sturdiest and went inside to wait out the storm. There was some wood laying around and a couple of the guys had matches. We made a fire and then tried to distract ourselves by talking and such."

"And was everyone still getting along at that point?"

"Mostly. We were all scared and soaked to the skin, so there was some tension. The conversation was mostly friendly until Rayleen leaned over and whispered something in Trevor's ear. He laughed and whispered something back that made Troy mad. They started to argue, but Jason told them to knock it off, so they left."

"Who left?"

"Troy and Rayleen."

"How long were they gone?"

"Troy came back after an hour or so, but Rayleen never did come back."

The answer to my next question would tell me quite a lot. "Did anyone else leave the group at that point?"

"Trevor left with Brooklyn. It seemed like they were going to find a place to make out."

"Even with a storm raging all around you?"

"Yeah, well, you don't know Trevor. He'd made it clear he'd planned the trip in the first place to get with Brooklyn and some storm wasn't going to stop him. Jason tried to get me to go off with him too, but I was too scared to leave the others. Eventually Jason got mad and left."

"And Katrina?"

"She was scared like me, so we started talking to Joshua, who was the only guy still by the fire until Troy came back."

I looked down at my pad and considered the notes I'd taken. "So Rayleen left with Troy during a fight. He came back, but she didn't. After they left but before Troy came back, Trevor went off with Brooklyn. Jason tried to get you to leave the building, but you wouldn't, so he took off alone."

"Sounds right."

I leaned forward and looked directly at Carrie, smiling and offering her a gesture of support. This next part was going to be hard and I wanted her to know I felt sorry about what I was about to put her through. "Okay, then what?"

"Then we heard a lightning strike that seemed like it was right on top of us. Troy, who was back by then, looked outside and said he thought it had hit a tree. He went to check it out. He came back a few minutes later and told us he'd found Rayleen's body next to the tree. She'd been stabbed to death."

I paused for a few beats to let Carrie get her emotions under control. "What did you do at that point?"

"We all ran out into the storm to see for ourselves whether Rayleen was dead and she was. Troy was totally pissed and took off into the storm, but Joshua and I went back inside. After a while we started to worry because no one else had come back inside. Eventually Joshua said he was going to go find out where everyone had gone off to."

I paused as I realized Carrie's account of events had begun to veer off from the reporting in the newspaper article I'd found. I tried to remember what I'd read; I was sure the newspaper had stated that after Rayleen's body was found the others split into small groups and went in search of the killer.

"You said you and Joshua went back to the building after Troy ran off. Where was Katrina?"

Carrie frowned. "I'm not sure. Maybe she went off. I thought I remembered everything clear as day, but now that I think about it, there was a time when it was just me and Joshua. No, I'm pretty sure Brooklyn was there too. Yes, I'm sure of it. She must have come back at some point."

"And Katrina?"

"I'm not sure. Maybe she left and came back. It was all so confusing. Anyway, I do remember it being me, Brooklyn, Katrina, and Jason by the fire after Joshua went to look for everyone."

I was beginning to think Carrie's eyewitness account wasn't going to help me in the least. Her memories were too fragmented.

"Okay, so you saw Rayleen's body. Troy ran off, but you and some of the others went back into the building. What did you do then?" The news article had said everyone fell asleep.

"Nothing. At least not until Troy came in and said Trevor was dead. We all freaked out, but Brooklyn totally lost it. She demanded to know where Troy had found Trevor. She said she needed to see for herself that he was dead. I tried to stop her, but she ran out into the storm. When she came back she told us that not only was Trevor impaled on an old ship's anchor but Joshua was dead too. He'd passed out and drowned."

"So at no point did *you* go out into the storm to look for your missing friends?"

Carrie started to cry. "No. I didn't go outside at all except when we found Rayleen. I was scared. We all were. We didn't know what to do. Three people were dead and the storm wasn't letting up. Jason was the most freaked out of anyone, I guess because the whole thing was his idea in the first place."

"At what point were all the survivors back together by the fire?"

Carrie paused to think about it. "After Troy said Trevor was dead or maybe it was after

Brooklyn said Joshua was dead. It seems like everyone was back by then. I might be a little confused about who left when, but by the end it was me, Jason, Troy, Brooklyn, and Katrina all huddled together by the fire, just praying the storm would let up by daybreak. Once it was light we headed back to Gull Island and notified the sheriff's office."

"Why didn't you just use the radio on the boat to call the authorities?"

"It wasn't working. I'm not sure why."

Based on Carrie's account, it sounded as if any of the survivors, other than Carrie herself, could have killed at least one of the victims. She claimed she never left the fire; everyone else was in and out, although, in all fairness, she was telling the story in a way that provided her own alibi. I'd need to speak to the others to see if their stories lined up.

"After you returned to Gull Island did you speak to a representative from the sheriff's office yourself?"

"Yes. There was a man asking questions."

"Did you tell him exactly what you just told me?"

Carrie hesitated. "I don't remember. I was in shock and my memory was playing tricks on me. Everything seemed jumbled and confused. After a while it seemed as if my memories became clearer, although now that I'm sitting here trying to tell you what happened, I realize I might not remember as much as I thought. I'm sorry to be so confusing."

I smiled. "You're doing fine. You went through a horrible experience. It's natural that things would get jumbled up a bit."

I jotted down a few additional notes. "Let's talk about Katrina's trip to Gull Island last week. Did you know she was coming?"

"No. She left the island right after we got back from the sailing trip. We didn't stay in touch. I haven't seen or talked to her since she left."

"You know there's a theory that she committed suicide by jumping off the pier?"

Carrie frowned.

"Does that sound like something she would do?"

Carrie paused before she answered me, appearing to give the question serious consideration. "I don't know; maybe. I told you, she mainly kept to herself, didn't have any close friends. We were all really upset after everything that happened, but I hadn't seen her in eleven years. Still, it seems strange that she'd come back here if she planned to kill herself."

"Some people think she committed suicide the way she did because she felt guilty for what occurred on the island."

"You think Katrina killed Rayleen, Trevor, and Joshua?"

I hesitated. "I don't have an opinion at this point about who might have killed them, but Katrina as the killer is a theory I intend to explore. What do you think? Could she have done it?"

Carrie bit her lip and didn't answer right away. "Could she have done it? I guess. Now that

I think about it, she was in and out of the building where we took refuge. And she was certainly strong enough. She worked out all the time and was in really good shape. Would she have done it? I don't see why. She never said she held a grudge against any of the others. In fact, I don't think she really knew any of them. I was the one who invited her."

"I know you said you didn't stay in touch with Katrina after she left Gull Island. Do you know if anyone else did?"

Carrie shrugged. "I don't think so. She was really traumatized about what happened. We all were, but she really seemed to lose it when we got back. I suppose you can ask the others."

That was exactly what I intended to do.

Chapter 4

I decided my next interview would be with Jason Rogers. His father had owned the boat the group sailed on and might remember more about everything that had happened. Jason was a marine mechanic who worked over at the marina in the summer, rounding out his income by doing odd jobs for Troy Wheeler during the off-season. October was a shoulder season on the island, so I wasn't sure where I could find him. I hoped his phone number might be listed and planned to look him up. My other option was to go over to the bank to ask Troy if he knew where he was. Of all the survivors, I knew Troy best; he'd helped me transfer my accounts when I'd moved to the island. As a matter of fact, speaking to Troy next might just be a good idea. He had gone on the trip as Rayleen's date. If they'd been dating perhaps he'd have some insight into what was going on in her life at the time of her death.

Of course I considered Troy a strong suspect as well.

I was pondering whether to head to the bank first when my stomach growled, reminding me that I hadn't eaten anything that day. I could go back to Gertie's, but the Burger Bar was closer, so I changed direction toward the little section of the island referred to as Town.

I ordered, then looked around the room, noticing Mayor Betty Sue Bell sharing a table with another woman. Betty Sue, who had big hair, outrageous clothes, and owned a hair salon as well as serving as the island's mayor, waved to me, indicating I should join them. It seemed both Gull Island natives were friendly and talkative, and I figured they'd make interesting lunch companions, so I walked across the restaurant.

"Barbara Jean, have you met Jillian Hanford?" Betty Sue asked.

"No," the buxom woman, with hair equally as big as Betty Sue's, answered. "I'm happy to meet you."

"Barbara Jean owns the bike rental and repair shop," Betty Sue explained.

"The place on Cove Street?" I asked.

Barbara Jean nodded.

"I considered dropping in over the summer to ask about a long-term rental, but I got so busy with the remodel that I never did."

Barbara Jean wiped her long bangs from her forehead as she smiled at me. "I heard Garrett had a long-lost sister who was going to take over the resort now that he's unable to do it himself. I understand you used to live in New York where you worked as a newspaper reporter."

"Yes. When Garrett approached me about taking over the management of the resort until he could work out a permanent solution, I decided to move to Gull Island temporarily to give it a try."

"So you've totally given up reporting?"

"No. I'm doing freelance work when I can get it and working on the novel I always wanted to write."

"Oh, and how is that going?"

"Slowly. I'll have more time to work on the novel once the renovations are completed. So far we're right on schedule with that. Three of the cabins are done and almost ready for occupants and another three cabins are in the process of renovation."

"Do you plan to fix up all twenty?" Barbara Jean asked.

"Eventually. We started with the cabins that were farthest away from the beach because we didn't want to disturb the turtles during nesting season. Now that's over, so I hope to begin work on the others as well. If all goes as planned we'll have all twenty cabins ready for spring."

Barbara Jean took a sip of her sweet tea before continuing. "I understand you're renting specifically to other writers?"

"That's my plan. I guess we'll see how it goes. I have five writers living in the main house at the moment who plan to move into cabins as they're ready. They're planning to live there full-time. Once the others are ready I'm planning to lease them to writers who need a place to work in solitude on a month-to-month basis."

Barbara Jean waved to the waitress for a refill of her sweet tea. "It sounds like that could work. I guess if you don't have enough interest from writers you can always go back to running the resort as a destination for families, like Garrett did."

"That's my backup plan," I admitted.

"So how's that brother of yours?" Betty Sue asked. "I understand he's back on the island and living out at Colin's place."

Colin Walton ran the Gull Island Senior Home. Garrett was only in his late fifties, quite a bit younger than the other occupants of the home, but he and Colin had been friends for a long time and Colin had made a place for him after he'd had his stroke.

"He's doing really well, considering the extent of the damage from the stroke. I doubt he'll ever have the strength or range of motion he once did, but he's improved quite a bit and his frame of mind has improved as well."

"I'm sure it must be hard for him to realize he's no longer able to run the resort," Betty Sue commented. "That land has been his whole life for a lot of years. It was so nice of you to give up your career in the city and come to the island to take over."

"I was happy to help Garrett out at least temporarily. I do miss New York and the faster way of life, but I guess in many ways I was ready for a change of scenery. I've never lived so close to the water before. I find I'm quite enjoying it."

"You do have an ideal location right there on the beach," Barbara Jean said.

"Are you getting comfortable in Town?" Betty Sue asked. "I know it can be hard to reestablish yourself after a move."

"I've been pretty busy with the renovations so I haven't had the opportunity to meet a lot of people yet, but I'd really like to. I've considered joining a group or maybe volunteering."

"Has anyone spoken to you about participating in the annual harvest festival?"

"No. This is the first I've heard of it."

"It's the last weekend in October," Betty Sue informed me as the waitress set my burger in front of me. "It's a big event that brings a whole passel of visitors to the island. You should volunteer for the committee. Participating in the event will be a good way to help out the community and meet some very nice people."

"I'd like that. When's the next meeting?"

"Tomorrow night at seven-thirty in the community center."

"Okay," I said. "I'll be there."

"And if you decide you'd like to trim up your pretty long hair stop by Betty Boop's," Betty Sue suggested. "I'll give you a trim and blowout on the house."

I touched my long braid. When I'd lived in the city I'd had my hair trimmed and shaped on a regular basis, but since moving to the island all I'd done was pull it back in a braid or ponytail. "I do need a trim," I admitted.

"Come on by anytime. I have an opening at three if you have time this afternoon."

"Actually, I'm taking Blackbeard for his twice-weekly visit with Garrett this afternoon, but maybe next week."

"Just give me a holler when you're ready. I'll fit you in someplace."

"Thank you. I really appreciate that. Oh, and as long as I've run into you, I was hoping to track down Jason Rogers. I want to speak to him about some odd jobs I need doing," I improvised. "I wonder if you might know where I can find him."

"Jason is up north visiting his mama," Betty Sue informed me. "I'm not sure when he'll be back. I can give you the names of some other handymen if it can't wait."

"It can wait," I answered. "But thank you for your offer." I looked at my watch. "I should be going."

"But you barely ate any of your hamburger," Barbara Jean said.

I looked down at the mostly intact sandwich. "I guess I wasn't that hungry after all. Maybe I'll just get a box and take it with me."

If I left now I could stop by to chat with Troy before it was time to take Blackbeard to see Garrett. I was disappointed I'd have to wait to speak to Jason, but I didn't feel I had time to waste, so I'd move on to whomever was available.

******

The Gull Island Bank was small, with just two tellers and the manager. I half-expected to find Troy manning the counter, as he often did when it was busy or he needed to give one of the tellers a break, but today he was conveniently alone in his office.

"I'd like to speak with Mr. Wheeler," I informed the tall, redheaded teller.

"Do you have an appointment?"

"No, but he doesn't look busy."

She turned around and looked in through the window at her boss's office. "Just one moment. I'll let him know you'd like to speak to him. Can I have your name?"

"Jillian Hanford."

"Please wait here. I'll be just a moment."

I waited while she poked her head in through the office door. He looked up and then out at me before eventually agreeing to see me. It was surprising he was already a bank manager considering he was, based on my research, only twenty-eight. Of course this was a teeny, tiny local bank, so there might not have been a lot of competition for the job.

"You can go on in," the teller informed me when she returned to the lobby.

"Thank you."

She opened the little gate that separated the lobby from the office area, allowing me access to the short hallway.

"How can I help you, Ms. Hanford?" Troy asked after I sat down on the other side of his desk. "Do you have additional assets to transfer?"

"No. I'm here today in my role as a reporter."

"I see," he said with a confused expression on his face. "Are you writing an article about small local banks?"

"No, the article isn't about banks; it's about murder. The Friday the Thirteenth Massacre, to be precise. I understand you were one of the teens who were on the little island when Rayleen Oswald, Trevor Bailey, and Joshua Vanderbilt died."

Troy's face turned red. "I hardly think this is the appropriate place to discuss that."

I ignored his comment. I didn't feel the same need to tread lightly with him as I had when I interviewed Carrie. "I understand that you were on the boat as Rayleen's date."

"I really must ask you to leave."

Yup; he was about to pop his lid. "I also understand you argued with Rayleen after the group sought refuge on Waverly Island. It seems the two of you left the structure where everyone else was huddled by the fire and were gone for quite some time. In fact, if my information is correct, Rayleen was never seen alive again."

"Look, I really must insist you go. I'm sure you have a job to do, but I'm a very busy man and this isn't the appropriate place for this conversation."

"It's my understanding Rayleen was flirting with another member of the group, which made you jealous."

"If you won't leave on your own I'll need to call security."

I wasn't worried. Partly because I'd never seen a security guard in the bank, but mostly because I almost had him. "Eyewitness accounts put you and only you out of sight of the others at the time Rayleen was killed."

"That's not true. I came back to the building where we were hanging out before the body was discovered. I was one of the people who went out to check out the tree when lightning struck it and found the body."

I smiled. *Gotcha*.

"So Rayleen was alive when you first returned to the structure where the others were waiting?"

"Yes. When we left the others, we argued about the way she was flirting with Trevor. She said I was being too possessive, and jealousy wasn't an attractive quality in a man. She suggested we break up. I told her to go to hell and she stomped off. I was mad, but I didn't kill her. I loved her."

"She just walked away in the middle of a storm?"

Troy took a deep breath. "I know that seems counterintuitive, but that's exactly what happened. Rayleen was very temperamental. She was a goddess in the sack but difficult to get along with anywhere else. She had a lot of really volatile mood swings that sometimes made her violent. I'd been the subject of her violent attacks enough times that I'd learned it was best to give her space to cool off, which is exactly what I did."

Interesting.

"And after you returned to the others?"

"I sat with them and tried to get my mind off Rayleen. I wasn't really worried about her, but I was upset. We'd fought before, a lot of times, but for some reason I was really angry then. I think the storm put everyone on edge."

"Do you remember who was by the fire when you returned to the group?"

Troy frowned. "I remember Carrie was there. She was talking to Brooklyn's cousin, Joshua. It seems like Jason was there too. I'm not sure if Trevor and Brooklyn were with us, but I'm pretty sure Katrina wasn't."

"And who discovered Rayleen was dead?"

"Me. I'd gone to see what the lightning hit and found Rayleen's body propped up against the tree that had been struck. I ran back to tell the others. They all went back out with me."

"And after you found Rayleen's body?"

"I totally flipped out. I took off into the woods with a wild idea that some random homicidal killer was responsible and I was going to hunt him down and make him pay for what he did to my girl."

I paused as I considered this, which was similar to what Carrie had said but dissimilar to the article I'd read. Again, I found it interesting. "I read an article in the local newspaper at the time that said all of you split up and went off to look for the killer. It made it sound as if an organized search had been executed, but you're saying you took off by yourself rather than joining a search team."

Troy put his hands on the back of his head and rested his forehead on his desk. I could see he was both angry and frustrated. I had him right where I wanted him.

"Look, I don't know what the others did after we found Ray. I took off and walked around in the rain, burning off my anger. In the course of that walk, I found Trevor's body. He'd been impaled on an old ship's anchor. I went back to tell the others. Everyone was understandably horrified. I can't remember exactly who did what at that point, I just remember feeling the terror you feel when you realize your nightmare is real."

"The newspaper article said that after Rayleen's body was found you all went back to the fire and fell asleep. Then Brooklyn noticed Trevor wasn't with you and went looking for him. The article indicates she was the one who found him."

"Yeah, well, the article is wrong. It happens, you know. People remember things differently."

"I suppose you're right about that. Do you have any idea who killed your friends?"

Troy shook his head, looking absolutely certain of his response. "None. I've gone over it again and again in my mind. The whole thing was like a bad horror movie. I kept hoping it was all some elaborate prank, but it wasn't. I can't imagine anyone who was on that little island that day could be capable of such a thing. If you'd been there you'd know how truly terrible it was." Troy looked me in the eye. "When I found Trevor's body his eyes were open and he had a look of absolute horror on his face. I couldn't sleep for months without seeing that face. Every time I closed my eyes there he was—looking at me."

I was beginning to feel bad for Troy, but I couldn't let up quite yet. There was one more thing I needed to ask. I adjusted my position in my chair so I could closely watch his face as I spoke. "Katrina Pomeroy killed herself. There are those who think she did it because she was overcome with guilt after killing her friends on the island."

I had to admit Troy looked shocked.

While I had been aggressively asking questions before, now I waited for Troy to make the next move. Finally, after at least a full minute he spoke. "You think Katrina killed Rayleen, Trevor, and Joshua?"

"Someone did. Do you have a better suspect in mind?"

I watched his face as he appeared to have an ah-ha moment, which he quickly masked. "No," he replied. "I have no idea who might have killed those kids. I can assure you, however, that it wasn't me. Now, if you'll excuse me, I need to get back to work."

I stood up. I'd gotten what I came for. "Thank you for your time."

As I left the office I turned for a moment to see Troy dialing the phone.

I decided it was time to fill in my new partner, Deputy Savage, on what I'd learned, and while I was there I'd casually ask him to put a trace on Troy's call, which had been made from a bank phone. If I was correct in my assumption that Troy had realized who the killer was, all we needed to do was see who he'd called and take our investigation from there.

Unfortunately, when I arrived at Savage's office he was out, and leaving a message like this on his voice mail didn't seem right, so I'd have to wait to assuage my curiosity. I asked the receptionist for a piece of paper and left a message for the deputy, stating that I had a possible lead and asking him to call me at his earliest opportunity. When he called I could tell him about Troy's desperate phone call. I glanced at the time, so we could narrow down which call originating from the bank was most likely to be the one Troy had made. It seemed obvious to me that he had a suspect in mind and I intended to find out who that was.

Back in my car, I realized I was almost out of gas, so I swung into the station in the middle of Town. I filled the tank, then stopped in the little store to grab a diet soda and use the restroom. When I returned to my car I found someone had left a note tucked under the windshield wiper. I took it with me and slipped into the car. There, I opened the note, which consisted of four words written in black crayon: *Leave well enough alone.*

Chapter 5

"Man overboard, man overboard," Blackbeard said to Garrett when I took him to the senior home later that day. When Garrett had had his stroke, it was Blackbeard who'd called Deputy Savage. Garrett had an old, corded phone, and when he'd fallen to the floor, the brilliant bird had knocked the receiver off the base and used his beak to peck at the speed-dial buttons Garrett had set up. He happened to connect with Savage, who'd come running after Blackbeard shouted, "Man overboard" into the handset. Since then, every time Blackbeard saw Garrett, those were the first words he said. Garret believed he was still saying it to show he knew why he'd moved into the senior home rather than coming home to the resort.

"It's good to see you, Blackbeard," Garret answered. "Is Jill taking good care of you?"

"Murder and mayhem, murder and mayhem."

Garrett glanced at me.

"The gang and I are investigating the Friday the Thirteenth Massacre and Blackbeard has been attending our meetings," I explained.

"I heard one of the survivors died the other day. That really was a tragedy."

"You were living on the island back then. Do you remember anything specific about the murders?"

Garrett tilted his head to the side, as if to access a long-buried memory. "I remember the entire island was up in arms. No one knew who had killed those kids or if the killer was still out there, waiting to kill again. There were a few newspaper articles, but it seemed as if there were several differing accounts about what had happened. I'm not sure the sheriff ever did manage to separate out fact from fiction."

"I read one of the articles and it does differ quite a bit from what I've learned from the survivors I've managed to speak to so far. I suppose that isn't all that odd, given the fact that those kids had to have been completely traumatized. I'm surprised Katrina Pomeroy was the only one who left Gull Island."

"The island is home to several generations of families who have built their lives and planned their futures here. When tragedy occurs you don't give up everything you've worked for and run away; you deal with things the best you can and move on."

I glanced at Blackbird, who was watching Garrett speak from his perch on his shoulder. It was too bad the senior home didn't allow pets.

Blackbeard and I got along okay, but I could tell he really missed Garrett.

"How's Dad doing?" I asked Garrett about the man who had sired us both but raised neither of us.

"Not well," Garrett answered. Our father had dementia and had been experiencing more bad days than good ones as of late.

"I'm sorry to hear that. I barely know him at all, but the two of you have just found each other and hoped for more time."

Garrett's mother had told him that his father, Max, had died when he was only six. Until recently Garrett had believed that to be true. During one of his coherent spells Max had come to Gull Island, and they'd been able to reconnect. Actually, that was how Garrett and I met. Max had told Garrett he had a daughter, Garett a half sister he'd never known existed. Although Garrett was twenty years my senior, we hit it off right away and he'd felt confident in asking me to help him. I had every intention of finding a way back to my life in New York, but in the meantime the island was a nice place to live while I waited for my next big break, so I'd agreed to Garrett's proposal on a temporary basis. I knew he was hoping I'd fall in love with the island and want to stay, but as much as I was enjoying myself, I highly doubted that would be the case.

"I'm happy we had the time we did," Garrett said. "We had a few good weeks together. I feel like it was enough if that's all we ever have. And who knows? Things could turn around again."

"I hope so."

"It was strange to know my father was alive after all those years of believing he was dead. At first I was angry with my mother for fabricating such a huge lie, but after thinking about it I realized she was just trying to protect me. I wish she was still alive so I could ask her all the questions I now have." Garrett glanced at me. "I'd like to meet your mother. I can't help but be curious about her. Do you think she'll ever come to the island?"

"I'll definitely introduce you if she comes for a visit, but I sort of doubt she will."

My mother, Miranda Monroe, was a flamboyant and successful actor who'd been off on location most of my growing-up years, leaving me to be raised by a series of nannies. Max had been out of the picture by the time I was four, and I didn't miss his presence in my life much, although I'd always been curious about him.

"Jack came by for a nice long visit yesterday," Garrett informed me.

"He did?" Jack and Garrett had met recently, when Jack had interviewed Garrett for an article he was writing for the *Gull Island News*. Despite the age difference, they seemed to have become friends.

"He brought a stack of books he thought I'd like. I never used to be much of a reader, but now I have all this free time, I've started reading quite a lot."

"Did Jack bring you any of his own books?"

"A couple. He's a talented storyteller. And how's the book you're writing coming along?"

"Slowly. I'll have more time to work on it when the remodel is done."

"Are we still on track to finish by spring?"

"It looks like it. The first three cabins are just about ready for Charles, Alex, and Brit to move into. The second set of three should be done in a month or so. I know Victoria would like to have her own cabin, and I already have a waiting list of writers who want to enter into short-term leases."

"That's wonderful. I guess renting to permanent and long-term guests will be easier than finding folks who just want to come for a weekend."

"A lot easier. In fact, with the list I have already I shouldn't even have to advertise for a while."

"Maybe you can move up the timeline a bit now that the turtles are gone," Garrett suggested.

"I've considered that, although I have some freelance work I'll need to juggle to make the time. I'm doing an article on the death of Katrina Pomeroy and how it might relate to the deaths of the three teenagers eleven years ago."

"I heard she was pushed off the pier during low tide and landed on the rocks below."

"She may have jumped."

"Walk the plank, walk the plank," Blackbeard, who seemed to have been listening intently, joined into the conversation.

Garrett chucked. "I supposed it might have looked that way, but how do you know?"

"Blackbeard got out when I was bringing in groceries on Friday. He flew away but came back after a couple of hours. I wonder if he saw what happened to Katrina."

"He might have. It certainly wouldn't be the first time he's gotten out and come home with a tale to tell."

"He really does seem to communicate and not just parrot words. Clara thinks he's been possessed by a ghost."

"I don't know about that, but he certainly isn't your average bird. If he helps you figure out what happened to Katrina it won't even be the first time he's helped out in a murder investigation."

Garrett had already explained to me how some friends of his had solved a murder Blackbeard had witnessed, finding a way to communicate what he'd seen.

After I left the senior center I drove to the market to pick up a few things I'd need for dinner. It was a cool day, so leaving Blackbeard in the car for a couple of minutes wouldn't be a problem. I'd been thinking about what to make ever since I'd invited Jack to come by and had finally decided on a menu with a Mexican theme.

"I'll just be a minute," I said to Blackbeard as I parked near the entrance to the small island grocery. "Please just wait quietly and don't get into any trouble. I'll bring you a cracker if you're good."

"Who's a good boy, who's a good boy?"

"I hope you are. Now sit tight."

I made sure all the doors were locked before I headed inside. Blackbeard was in a travel carrier, but I didn't want someone to happen by, see the bird, open the door, and let him out. It was one thing when Blackbeard got out at home. He knew where he lived and how to get back there. I wasn't sure he'd be able to find the house if he got out in some other location. When I'd first moved in Blackbeard had gotten out all the time. I'd never had a pet before and wasn't used to having to remember to do things like keep the doors closed. The longer I lived with the talkative bird the better I was at taking note of his presence throughout the day.

"Blackbeard stopped by the other day," the clerk informed me as I was checking out.

"He came all the way over here?"

"Yup. The front door was open and he flew inside, landed on the checkout counter, and asked me for a cracker. I gave him one. I hope that was okay."

I added a couple of packs of gum to the counter. "Yeah, that was fine. I had no idea he could cover so much territory in just a couple of hours."

"He's a bird. I imagine he can cover a lot of ground if he's inclined to do so. If you ask me, he knows exactly where he wants to go before he even leaves home."

"You think so? I always figured he just flew around randomly."

"Maybe, but it seems to me he has a plan with specific places he wants to go. After I gave him the cracker he took off out the door. I was going to call to let you know he was here, but he managed to escape before I had the presence of mind to try to catch him."

"Did he say anything else while he was here?" I wondered. "Anything other than asking for the cracker?"

"He made a comment about grog and wenches and then something about walking the plank."

"Grog and wenches is what he says when he goes to Sully's," I said, referring to a local bar to which Garrett had taken him before he had his stroke. It seemed the folks who frequented the place got a kick out of him and his saucy talk. It occurred to me to take him to Sully's now, to see if he said anything to him. I was already half-convinced Blackbeard's talk of walking the plank referred to Katrina going to the end of the pier and jumping in.

"That'll be fifty-two twenty-six," the clerk informed me.

I ran my credit card, thanked the man, and headed back to the car. I gave Blackbeard a cracker, then asked him if he wanted to stop by Sully's on the way home.

"Grog and wenches, grog and wenches."

"It'll need to be a quick trip; we're having company for dinner."

"Captain Jack, Captain Jack."

"Yes, Captain Jack is coming." I wasn't sure why he called him Captain Jack, though he did tend to add the captain designation to the men he was fondest of, and Blackbeard adored Jack.

It was early for the bar crowd, so Sully's wasn't busy. As I walked in, I saw two men at the bar watching a football game; other than Sully and them, the place was deserted.

"Blackbeard," Sully greeted the bird.

"Who's a good boy, who's a good boy?"

"Blackbeard's a good boy," Sully said before handing him a cracker. Then he looked at me. "You here for a drink?"

"No. I need to get home. I just wanted to ask you if Blackbeard was here on Friday. He got out while I was bringing in the groceries."

"Yeah, he stopped by. It was earlier in the day and there wasn't anyone around. I was in the back working on the books when he flew in and asked for a cracker."

"Did he say anything else?"

"Yeah, he was in a chatty mood that day. He was only here for about ten minutes before he flew away again, but he talked nonstop the entire time. He seemed sort of worked up."

"Do you remember what he said?"

Sully paused. "He mentioned something about someone walking the plank. Princess Anna; that was it."

Princess Anna was a character in a movie Blackbeard and I had watched the other week. Princess Anna had long blond hair. I wondered if Katrina Pomeroy had long blond hair as well. I'd have to verify my hunch, but the fact that Blackbeard was talking about Princess Anna on the same day he was talking about walking the plank really did make it seem as if he'd witnessed Katrina's death.

"Did he say anything else?"

"Like I said, he was chatty that day." Sully raised his hand to his chin and squinted just a bit. "I wasn't paying all that much attention to what he was saying. I'm sure he made some other comments, but at the moment I can't remember what they were. Is it important?"

"I'm not sure. I think Blackbeard might have seen Katrina Pomeroy when she was in town on Friday."

"The girl who died?"

"Yeah. If he did see something I'm curious as to what it was. Blackbeard doesn't usually ramble random words. I think he really tries to communicate with people using the words he knows. If I had to guess, he saw what happened to Katrina and came over here to tell you about it."

"But I wasn't paying attention. Dang. I'm sorry I didn't give him my full attention. Do you think he might have gone to tell someone else because I wasn't listening?"

"He stopped by the market, but he wasn't as chatty while he was there." I looked at Blackbeard. "Did you see a girl fall off the pier when you were out the other day?"

"Princess Anna, Princess Anna."

"Yes, Princess Anna. Did you see what happened to her?"

"Walk the plank, walk the plank."

"Yes, she walked to the end of the pier and then fell into the water. Was there anyone else with her?"

"Pickles and cream, pickles and cream."

I glanced at Sully, who shrugged. What in the heck could Blackbeard mean by that?

Chapter 6

Tonight the mood at the house was light and festive, while the previous evening had been masked in gloom and darkness. Blackbird sat on his perch telling each of my dinner companions to drink hearty every time I poured the margaritas I'd prepared to go along with my Mexican-themed dinner consisting of chicken and beef burritos and cheese enchiladas.

"Do we have any more salsa?" Brit asked after I'd set up the make-your-own-burrito bar.

"In the pantry. You may as well get some more chips too."

"It looks like your burrito bar is a hit. I haven't tried one yet, but everyone is raving about the beef. You'll have to give me the recipe."

"You cook?" I'd be surprised if she did. Brit was a sweet girl, but she seemed to be permanently plugged into her phone and other electronic devices and to this point had never demonstrated an interest in anything other than making a mark in social media.

"Me?" Brit snickered. "No. The recipe is for my mom and, someday, my personal chef."

I laughed. "I guess it's good to plan ahead. Have you seen Alex?"

"Out on the patio with the guy from the newspaper—who, by the way, is a real babe. Is he single?"

"He is, although I didn't peg him as your type."

"My type? Lord no. He's totally old. I was thinking of my mother again."

"You do know who Jack is?"

"Yeah. You told me. The guy who owns the newspaper."

"Well, yes, he does own the newspaper, but he also writes novels under his full name."

Brit glanced in his direction. Her expression showed slightly more interest. "So what's his name?"

"Jackson Jones."

Brit's jaw dropped. "Shut up! That's Jackson Jones?"

"In the flesh."

"But Jackson Jones is a huge name. He has millions of dollars. Tens, maybe even hundreds of millions. What is he doing on this tiny island?"

"Same thing as you: following his dream. You were a business major who wanted to be a writer and he was a writer who wanted to own a newspaper."

Brit just shook her head. "Well, if that doesn't beat all. I'm having dinner with Jackson Jones. Wait until I tell my friends."

She pulled out her phone, I imagined to post her news on one or more social network sites.

"Jack is just Jack on the island. Why don't we respect his privacy? I'm sure the last thing he wants is to have a bunch of fans pounding on his door."

Brit looked disappointed, but she didn't argue.

"Go grab those chips," I said.

After Brit left for the kitchen I went out on the deck to tell the guys they'd best come in to eat before the food got cold. Alex headed inside, but Jack lingered.

"It sure is a beautiful evening," he commented as the waves created by high tide rolled onto the shore.

"It really is. I can't believe we were in the middle of the storm of the decade this time last night."

"It's true a day can make a big difference. Did you manage to get through it without any major damage?"

"We seem to have. At least I didn't find anything, although I haven't had the chance to check all the cabins. The building inspector is coming in the morning to give his final approval on the three cabins, so I hope none of them sustained any damage. The natives are getting restless. It'll be better when everyone has their own space."

"You told me you have five houseguests, but you only have three cabins," Jack pointed out.

"Charles, Alex, and Brit are taking the first three. Clara says she's just as happy in the main house and my friend Victoria travels a lot and is almost never here, so they're both more than happy to wait for another phase in the project. How about your mansion on the bluff? You all moved in?"

"I am."

"Don't you get lonely, rambling around that great big house all by yourself?"

"I don't mind being alone, but I have been thinking about maybe getting a pet."

"I never had a pet before Blackbeard, but I'm enjoying his company. I feel as if I can have a conversation with him. Today he told me a story about Princess Anna walking the plank."

"Princess Anna?"

I explained the way Blackbeard communicated, and that I believed he was trying to tell us that he'd seen Katrina Pomeroy fall from the pier. "I guess that makes sense."

"There's more. When I asked if there was anyone with Princess Anna when she walked the plank he said pickles and cream."

Jack frowned. "What does that mean?"

"Honestly, I have no idea. They aren't foods you often find paired and Blackbeard doesn't eat either of them. I don't think he was being literal. Maybe the person he saw wore green clothes and looked like a pickle. Or maybe he was eating a pickle. Or maybe pickle is just some random word. I'm not sure what Blackbeard is trying to say, but if he did see someone with Katrina that might eliminate the suicide theory."

"It seems like it might be important enough for us to see if we can figure out exactly what Blackbeard saw."

"I agree. It's one of the things on my list, which keeps getting longer and longer. We plan to discuss the case as a group after dinner, but I did want to ask you about newspaper articles. The one I have from the local paper seems to be inconsistent with what the survivors I've had a chance to speak to have told me. I don't know if the person who wrote it was lazy or incompetent, or maybe he wrote the article after speaking to only one source, but it isn't lining up. I was wondering if you could track down any articles written about the Massacre right after it happened eleven years ago. Additional articles published in the local paper, or articles published in other newspapers off Gull Island. It was a pretty big deal. I'd be willing to bet the murders even received some national news attention."

"I'll see what I can find," Jack promised.

"In the meantime, I'll be bringing it up tonight. Maybe one of the others knows something that could help explain the discrepancy."

Jack glanced toward the house. "If we want to get any food before it's gone we'd best head inside."

"Right behind you."

******

After dinner Charles set up the large white board the group used as an investigation tool. We'd used it in the past to jot down notes, display newspaper articles and sticky notes, and generally provide a way to map things out in the hope of finding links and patterns that would allow us to pull everything together. In addition to Jack, we were the same group who'd assembled on Saturday. Everyone had done something to work on the case, even if it was just looking stuff up online, so we went around the room, each saying what we'd found out, before opening up the floor for discussion.

Charles was ready with a marker in hand, having volunteered to record what was said, so we asked him to go first.

"Because I had been a frequent visitor to the island for a number of years before moving here, I know quite a few folks who were around here back then. I decided to ask around to try to get a general impression of the kids who were involved in the Friday the Thirteenth Massacre. Opinions, as they usually are, were varied, but most agreed on a couple of things I found somewhat important."

We all waited quietly for Charles to continue.

"The first thing I found interesting was the opinion of the character of the first victim, Rayleen Oswald. It seems she was not popular. According to pretty much everyone I spoke to, she could be harsh and cruel. The consensus seemed to be that she was a bully who used her looks and sexuality to get what she wanted. She was not above tearing others down along the way

78

and most felt she probably got what she deserved."

"She must have been pretty bad to deserve to be stabbed thirteen times," I said.

"It sounds like she was. Not only did she physically, verbally, and emotionally abuse her peers but she was responsible for a very popular teacher at the school being fired. It seemed he flunked her, and when he refused to change her grade, she accused him of sexual assault. Her lie was convincing enough that the man lost his job."

"Wow, that is bad," I admitted. "What about the other kids?"

"Jason Rogers, the boy whose father owned the boat, was rich at the time, which caused him to be pompous and entitled. People liked to be around him because he was popular and wielded a certain amount of power, but no one, it seemed, actually liked him. When his father lost his money and Jason was forced to take on any sort of job he could, people on the island felt he was simply getting what he deserved."

"That's two for two in terms of the teens 'getting what they deserved,'" I pointed out.

"Yes, that was a popular theme." Charles paused before he continued. "Trevor Bailey, the second victim, was known as a snitch. He was a talented athlete, which made him popular to a degree, but he wasn't above ratting out his peers if it served his purposes. According to the people I spoke to, Trevor was responsible for more than one athlete being kicked off the team because he reported their actions to his mother, who was on the school board. There are some who felt he was justified in doing what he did, while others saw his action as self-serving; in each instance he was promoted to the first-string position previously held by the team member he snitched on."

"Sounds like a real jerk," Alex commented.

"Maybe. Again, there seem to be people who felt Trevor got what he deserved."

"And the others?" I asked.

"Most people I spoke to thought Troy Wheeler was a needy, sniveling nerd who was way out of his league dating Rayleen. The consensus is that he hasn't changed a bit over the years."

I had to admit I'd had the same impression of him when I'd met with him that afternoon. "If the islanders see Troy as a needy nerd how did he make it onto the town council? It's an elected positon."

"While I got the impression that most of the people I spoke to don't particularly care for Troy as a person, as the bank manager he wields a lot of power. One of the men specifically told me that during the last election he worked on Troy's campaign, not because he thought he was the best man for the job but because a loan he really needed to expand his business was under review and it would be Troy who had final say as to whether he would get it."

"I guess that makes sense. What about the others?"

"Brooklyn Vanderbilt was a popular girl in high school: cheerleader, homecoming queen, and so forth," Charles continued. "She seems to be generally well liked these days as well. I spoke to quite a few people and everyone had nice things to say about her."

He cleared his throat before he moved on. "Katrina Pomeroy was a serious artist who was known for being dark and moody. It was said she suffered from clinical depression rather than just teenage angst. She was a loner who didn't have many friends. Most of the people I spoke to felt she was only on the sailing trip because Carrie invited her. Other than Brooklyn, Carrie Quincy seems to be the nicest of the bunch. It appears she's popular among the islanders, and Gertie went on and on about what a sweet and giving soul she is."

"And Joshua?" I asked.

"Joshua Vanderbilt was a visitor to the island, unknown to those I spoke to."

"Thank you, Charles. I'm not sure that helps us when it comes to solving this mystery, but I suppose understanding the dynamic between the eight kids who were on the trip could come in handy at some point in the future." I turned to Alex, who was sitting next to Charles.

"Brit and I teamed up to cover social media," he responded. "I took a look at everyone's current footprint and Brit dug into the past."

Like Charles's information, I supposed the social media presence of each person involved could give us clues down the line, although again, I doubted it would help us to figure out who'd killed those three kids eleven years ago and how their deaths might relate to Katrina's.

"Before their Massacre both Rayleen and Brooklyn had Myspace pages that were dedicated to promoting themselves as individuals as well as for interacting with others," Brit began. "Both pages were focused on clothes, makeup, teen heartthrobs, that sort of thing. Based on the number of people who the girls interacted with, I assume they were both fairly popular, although Rayleen's popularity tended to be based on power gained by clawing her way to the top, whereas Brooklyn appeared to have genuine friends."

Brit took a breath and reviewed the notes she'd taken before she continued. "Troy Wheeler also had a Myspace page, which seemed to be a way to explore the science fiction and fantasy worlds he appeared to be hooked on. I didn't notice a lot of interaction with others or even a desire to engage others in any way. Troy seemed to be a bit of a loner and his page was focused on his own need to actively participate in his fantasies.

"Katrina Pomeroy also had a page, which I found the most interesting. Instead of posting to communicate with friends about the new makeup she'd just bought or the date she'd been on the previous night, she used her page to highlight her photography, as well as her very dark and very personal poetry. Death, suffering, and judgment were popular themes with her. I couldn't find pages for Carrie or any of the other guys, but that doesn't mean they didn't have them. They could very well have used different names for their pages."

I was beginning to see a pattern emerging. I looked at Alex.

"Currently, all the survivors have, or in Katrina's case, had, Facebook pages. Some have Twitter, Instagram, and Snapchat accounts as well. Katrina seemed to focus her social media presence on creating a brand for her art. While she'd evolved somewhat as an adult, her work had continued to have a dark, moody feel to it. She was becoming very popular and her gallery seemed to be doing well."

Alex added, "Brooklyn's social media presence is mostly about her kids and her family life. Her focus seems to be Facebook. I also found an Instagram account, but I didn't find accounts for Snapchat, Twitter, or any of the other more modern forms of social media. Carrie has a Facebook page that's focused on movies, television, music, and other forms of entertainment. She seems to engage in quite a bit of star envy and adoration.

"As for the guys," Alex continued, "Troy seems focused on portraying himself as a wealthy businessman, although I'm not sure he's as wealthy as he leads others to believe. There are no photos on his social media sites of friends or family, which led me to wonder if he has any. Jason has a Facebook page but rarely posts, and when he does, he's mostly reposting someone else's update."

I smiled at Alex before I turned to Clara. Her report had more to do with the vibrations she was picking up and feelings she had that she was trying to classify. I love Clara, I really do, but there were times when most of what she said had absolutely no real-world application.

Jack said he'd spoken to Katrina's sister, who'd had no idea she planned to visit Gull Island. She couldn't imagine why she would want to, when she'd continued to have nightmares about the Massacre. Jack had asked her opinion regarding the suicide theory, and she'd insisted that while Katrina definitely had a dark side, she couldn't imagine her ending her life, although she did admit Katrina had attempted suicide in the past. Jack had asked why, if Katrina had already tried to end her suffering once, she wouldn't do it again, and her sister had shared that even if her depression had progressed to the point where she would consider killing herself, she was certain she wouldn't do it on the island where, according to Katrina, her nightmares still lived.

"Of course the Massacre didn't occur on Gull Island," I said.

"That's true, and I made that point as well," Jack answered. "According to Katrina's sister, although the murders occurred on Waverly Island, there was something or someone on Gull Island Katrina was afraid of."

"It does seem odd she'd return to a place she'd fled if her intention was to kill herself," I mused. "The biggest thing I have to report are the inconsistencies I found between what the newspaper reported and what the witnesses I spoke to today told me. I didn't get the sense that either Carrie or Troy were necessarily lying, but if their memories of that night are accurate and they're telling the truth, things went down quite a bit differently from what we originally believed."

I spent the next twenty minutes outlining exactly what Carrie has shared with me. Troy's story was slightly different but closer to Carrie's than to the newspaper's. Jack mentioned that he was going to try to find news coverage of the murders from other sources, and Alex and Brit, our millennials, promised to dig around to see what they could find as well.

"I'm going to speak to both Brooklyn and Jason as soon as I get the chance," I added. "I'm interested to hear how their stories line up with Carrie and Troy's."

"When should we plan to meet again?" Brit asked.

"I'm going to attend the meeting for the harvest festival tomorrow, but Tuesday works for me."

The others said Tuesday would work for them as well.

"I have the final inspection on the first three cabins in the morning," I said. "If things go well, Charles, Alex, and Brit can start moving in right away."

The announcement met with smiles all around.

"Have you heard from Victoria?" Alex asked. "Will she be here as planned?"

"As far as I know, but perhaps I'll call her to check in."

The group began to break up, with everyone going their own way. Each of the bedrooms on the second floor had a sitting area and each of my houseguests had their own television and work area. Even though we lived together, we didn't spend all that much time together.

"We're both going to the planning meeting tomorrow; would you like to share a bite before?" Jack asked as he gathered his belongings in preparation for returning home.

"You're on the planning committee?"

"This will be my first meeting as well, but I'm looking forward to helping out. So how about it? Do we have a date?"

"I'll meet you for dinner, but this definitely won't be a date."

Jack frowned. "Is there someone else?"

"No. No one else. It's just that I promised myself when I was thirteen years old that I would never again date a guy named Jack."

He seemed puzzled.

"Jack and Jill," I said. "When I was thirteen I had a huge crush on a boy named Jack and it turned out he liked me back. I was in seventh heaven for about a day until the teasing began. Trust me when I say that although Jack was cute and sweet, being his girlfriend wasn't worth the harassment."

"You'd seriously refuse to date a man named Jack no matter how well suited you were for each other?"

"Yup."

"That's nuts."

I shrugged. "Maybe it is, maybe it isn't. But a promise to yourself is still a promise."

Chapter 7

Monday. October 16

Stan Barber wasn't a serious person, which seemed odd to me given the fact that he bore the title building *inspector*. It seemed to me someone with that word in his job title should be a bit more focused and intense than Mr. Barber appeared to be. Not only was he wearing a pair of filthy work boots with mismatched socks but he topped that with ratty shorts and an equally worn T-shirt. The most outrageous thing about him, however, was the hat, shaped like a turtle, perched on the top of his head. If I'd seen him in passing, I would assume he'd spent the day at the beach or possibly was among the homeless who camped out and lived on the public beaches in the area. Never in a million years would I guess he was the man who had the fate of the resort in his hands.

"Woo-wee, you sure do have yourself a nice spot here." Stan stood with his hands on his hips as he looked out over the resort.

"Thank you. I agree, it's an exceptional piece of property."

"Not a lot of places with the sand and sea on one side and the marsh on the other. This place is real special."

I had to agree with him. The resort was located on a peninsula on the south end of the island. Except for the road that accessed the resort, it was almost completely surrounded by water. When I'd first arrived on the island I'd been amazed at the variety of both plant and animal life that could be found right here in my own backyard.

"You know, this is one of the pre-mi-um turtle beaches on the island," the inspector informed me after walking right past the cabins he was there to inspect in favor of the little path that led down to a white sand beach.

"Yes, so I've been told. Are you involved with the turtle rescue group?"

"Second-generation turtle watcher. My mama was one of the founding members, God rest her soul. I'm surprised we haven't run into each other a time or two, with you living near a nesting beach."

"My arrival on the island was fairly abrupt after my half brother, Garrett, suffered a stroke. I came as quickly as I could once I learned he needed my help, but I still had commitments I needed to meet in my old life, so I was back and forth between Gull Island and New York until recently. I'm interested in the turtle rescue effort, however, and would like to be involved come next nesting season."

"You need to talk to Meg over at the museum. She can get you a hat and fill you in on everything you need to know."

"Hat?"

Stan pointed to his head. "All the rescue workers are given a hat as a thank-you for all we do."

"I see." I was sincere about helping out but was pretty sure a turtle hat wasn't going to work with my current wardrobe. "So, about the cabins we're looking to receive final clearance on... We replaced all the windows, as well as the exterior decks and siding."

Stan turned around so he was facing in the general direction of the cabins. "Yup. I can see that."

"I made sure the contractor followed the commercial specs for the decks because I plan to rent out the cabins."

"Seems like that might have been a good idea."

I waited for him to pull out a clipboard for his notes, a measuring tape to confirm that the security railing was the required height, possibly a camera to commit the changes we'd made to memory, but all he did was turn back toward the beach and start talking about the variety of birds that could be found on the island. I listened politely, not wanting to anger the man who had the power to grant or deny my permit, but I couldn't help but wonder how long he allotted himself for each job.

Thirty minutes had passed by the time he finally headed back to the cabins.

"I think you'll find that we used the best-quality materials on both the interior and exterior during the remodel process." I opened the door to the first cabin.

He stuck his head inside. "Uh-huh. The paint is a nice color, but you might want to rethink the carpeting on the floors."

"You aren't a fan of carpet?"

"Not when you live so close to the beach. Tile would provide a more durable surface."

"I see. I'll keep that in mind when I purchase flooring for the next phase of the remodel."

"I know a guy who can hook you up. He'll give you a good price."

"Thank you. I'll keep that in mind."

The inspector walked down the path and approached the second cabin. He opened the door and peeked inside. "That alder in the kitchen?"

"Yes. We had all new cabinets installed."

"I'm more of an oak man myself, but them are nice." He closed the door and took a step back. "Guess that'll do 'er."

"You're finished?" Surely his inspection would consist of more than a cursory look at the changes we'd made from a distance. "What about the third cabin?"

"Seen what I needed to." He walked over to the drive and opened the door to his truck. He leaned inside and took out a file folder. He opened the folder, took out a form, and handed it to me. "This here is your permit. You might want to keep it handy. Good luck with your endeavors, and don't forget to stop by the museum to speak to Meg. Livin' where you do, knowin' how to protect the turtles will be an important thing for you to have a handle on."

Was it really going to be this easy? I'd been stressing over this inspection for days. "Thank you. I'll stop by to speak to Meg. Maybe even later today. It was nice meeting you."

"You too. I'll be out again when you get the next three cabins done. Maybe I'll bring Gordo. He'd enjoy a tour of the place."

"Gordo?"

"Friend of mine who just got divorced after thirty years of marriage. Poor guy is down on his luck, so I'm lettin' him stay with me for a bit."

"I see. Yes, please do bring your friend for a tour. Anytime."

He tipped his turtle hat and climbed into his truck. I shook my head as he drove away. I knew island living usually equated to casual living, but Stan Barber was the most casual inspector I was certain I'd ever have the opportunity to cross paths with.

"How'd it go?" Charles walked out onto the drive from the main house after Stan left.

I held up the permit. "It looks like you're good to move in."

"Happy to hear that. It has been nice living in the big house, but I will be glad to have a space for myself."

"I understand completely. It's always nice to have a space where you can be yourself and unwind."

"Are you planning to work on your article today?"

"I hoped to interview the two survivors I haven't had a chance to speak to yet, but first I'm heading over to the museum to speak to a woman named Meg about a turtle hat. Do you want to come along?"

"I would love to, but I think I will start moving in. See you when you get back."

******

The museum had been built on a hill, which provided an unobstructed view of the ocean in the distance. Coupled with colorful flower gardens and well-maintained walkways, the grounds provided a pleasant place to gaze out at the sea or share a snack on one of the many picnic tables.

"Welcome to the Gull Island Museum," the woman, whose name tag read MEG COLLINS, greeted me as soon as I walked in. She looked to be in her midsixties and had neatly styled hair in a natural silver-gray color that almost matched the lightweight blouse she wore with darker gray slacks. "How can I help you today?"

"My name is Jillian Hanford. I moved to the island recently."

"I heard Garrett had a long-lost sister who had moved here to take over the resort. Welcome."

"Thank you. I hoped to find out a little bit about the island and to ask about the turtle rescue squad I understand you're in charge of."

"Please have a seat."

Meg motioned toward a table that was littered with several large photo albums and yellowed books. Once I was seated she began a narrative that was rehearsed yet informative.

"First off, you need to know that the Sea Islands, of which Gull Island is one, are a chain of tidal and barrier islands off the southeastern coast of the United States reaching from South Carolina to northern Florida. Gull Island is the easternmost in the chain, which, according to oral history, was originally settled by a group of pirates in the late seventeenth century. Other islands in the area were populated by indigenous people until the Spanish began to colonize them in the mid-seventeen hundreds. The peninsula where the resort is located is an important piece of property both from a historical perspective and an environmental one."

"Historical?"

"It's said that the peninsula was once the location of a settlement. One of the first in the area. Any infrastructure that may have existed is long gone, but there are those who believe there's all sorts of buried treasure left behind, just waiting to be found. The problem with that is that the island tends to attract a lot of treasure hunters intent on finding whatever it is the pirates who lived here prior to the Spanish might have left behind."

"I suppose treasure hunting helps to generate tourism dollars," I commented.

"It does. But it brings problems as well."

"What sort of problems?" I wondered.

"Digging, for one. Treasure hunters tend to dig, and when they dig on the beach they create obstacles for the newly hatched turtles as they make their way to the water. That's where our group comes in. We monitor the nests as well as the beaches in general during nesting season and mitigate any obstacles that may arise. If you're interested in joining our group I can give you some literature to look over."

"I'd like that. Thank you."

"Garrett was always so good about watching out for the turtles and other wildlife he felt he was charged with protecting. I felt so bad when I learned he wasn't going to be able to return to the resort. Not that I'm not happy to have you on the island, but I know what the resort means to him."

"I'm going to try my best to fill his shoes at least temporarily. Is there some sort of training that goes along with being a turtle rescue worker?"

"We do classes in the spring. Mostly you just need to know what's normal nesting behavior and what isn't so you can make a decision when to intervene and when to let nature take its course. The materials I'll give you will provide a good overview. Feel free to stop by again or call me with questions."

"Thank you. I will. Do you mind if I look around a bit?"

"Please do. Most everything in the museum was donated by local individuals or families."

I could already tell the collection housed in the museum was impressive. "It's been brought to my attention that there are many families living on the island that have been here for multiple generations."

"Many, many families. Gull Island is the sort of place that once you arrive you want to stay put. I understand you moved here from New York. Did you grow up there?"

"No. I more or less grew up nowhere and everywhere. My dad was out of the picture and my mom moved around a lot, so we never really settled in one place. I do like New York, however."

"I'm sure New York was exciting, but I think you'll really enjoy Gull Island. I understand you're still doing freelance writing."

"I am." I was surprised Meg knew that. I'd never met her before today, and I certainly hadn't mentioned it.

"Rick told me when we had dinner last night."

"Rick?"

"Deputy Savage."

"Is he your son?"

"No. Just a friend. I guess you could say I'm a surrogate mom of sorts. We try to have dinner one or two Sundays a month."

"That's nice. My mom and I aren't close, but I always thought it would be nice to have a family to spend holidays and share Sunday dinner with."

"Where does your mother live?"

"Los Angeles. She's in the entertainment industry, so, as I said, she travels a lot."

"Is your mother a singer? Or an actor?"

"An actor."

"Would she have been in anything I've seen?"

I shrugged. "Probably. Her name is Miranda Monroe."

"Miranda Monroe is your mother?"

"I'm afraid so."

"I've seen all her movies. She really is very talented. It seems, based on what I've read, that she's lived a fascinating life."

"That's Mom. Fascinating." I held up the pamphlet. "Thanks again for the information. I'll be sure to get back to you when I'm ready to formally join the group."

Chapter 8

I left the museum and decided to stop by the sheriff's office to see if Deputy Savage was in. He hadn't called me back the previous day, which didn't surprise me, but I still wanted to have a chat with him to, hopefully, find out who Troy had called the minute I walked out of his bank office the previous day. Getting Savage's cooperation wasn't going to be an easy thing, but any man who took time out of his life to have dinner on a regular basis with a sweet older woman must be a good guy. In my experience, good guys always came through in the end.

"Deputy Savage," I greeted as I entered his office and found him sitting at his desk.

"I had a feeling I'd be hearing from you today."

"Maybe you have a touch of psychic flare like my friend Clara."

Deputy Savage raised one eyebrow but didn't answer. I hadn't been offered a seat, but I decided to take one anyway, so I sat down on the chair across the desk from the man dressed in gray.

"I have several reasons for being here," I began. "The first has to do with the major inconsistencies I'm finding between the article I found in the local newspaper eleven years ago and the stories the survivors are telling me."

"You've been snooping around?"

"I was up-front about that from the beginning," I reminded him. "So about these inconsistencies...?"

"When the survivors returned to the island each was interviewed individually by the deputy assigned to Gull Island at the time. The survivors were obviously traumatized, but the stories they told were so different as to be deemed completely useless."

"Different how?"

"If we're going to continue this discussion it's to be understood that everything we discuss from this point forward is strictly off the record."

I frowned. Off the record would help to assuage my curiosity, but it would probably hinder my ability to write the article I wanted to write. Still, my guess was that Savage wouldn't share what he knew if I didn't agree.

"What if I discover something we discuss during this conversation on my own?"

Savage shook his head. "If we talk about something today it's strictly off the record regardless."

Smart. Savage didn't know what I already knew, but by agreeing to speak to me in return for my promise not to publish what we talked about he was planting himself firmly in the driver's seat. Not only were any new clues I might pick up on during the course of the conversation protected, but anything I already knew was protected if it came up now as well.

I shrugged. I really didn't have anything at this point, so I wasn't risking anything. "Okay, you have a deal. I promise not to publish whatever we discuss in my article unless you specifically agree to let me use it. However, if we don't discuss something, it isn't protected by our agreement."

Savage opened his desk drawer, took out a file folder, and handed me a report. I turned to the first page to find a transcript of what each of the survivors had to say on their return to Gull Island. The first thing I noticed was that the account of the events on October 13 eleven years ago by Brooklyn Vanderbilt matched the information printed in the newspaper almost exactly. It appeared as if the reporter had interviewed her, then run the story without speaking to the others.

Weird.

The second transcript had been provided by Carrie Quincy. The sequence of events she'd told me the day before was exactly what had been recorded in the report except for one thing: yesterday she'd told me Brooklyn had left the fire with Trevor, while in the report she'd stated Brooklyn was with her the entire time and neither of them ever left the others. I didn't have the sense she'd been lying to me and she'd admitted her memory was jumbled, so I supposed that could account for the difference in her story.

The next transcript had been provided by Jason Rogers. This was of particular interest because I had yet to speak to him and didn't know when he'd be back from his mama's, so I had no idea whether I'd be able to track him down before my article was due. His story started off the same as the one Carrie had told. A bunch of them had decided to cut school and go sailing, they'd lost track of time, and a storm had blown in before they could get home. Jason felt it was too dangerous to risk continuing and they'd pulled up on Waverly Island.

Jason's report continued with their finding shelter and making a fire, but that was where the similarity to Carrie's story ended. Carrie had said Trevor and Rayleen were flirting and Troy got mad. They'd started to argue and Jason told them to knock it off. Carrie had told me that was when Troy and Rayleen left the others, but according to Jason, Rayleen smacked Troy and told him to stop being such a weenie. He'd slapped her back, causing her to dig into their supply of rum punch and start drinking. The rum made her sick and she went outside to puke. She wasn't seen again until after the lightning struck the tree. Jason went out to see if the strike had started a fire and found Rayleen dead.

I paused to let that sink in. I was trying to picture in my mind exactly how each scenario had played out. If Carrie was correct, Troy and Rayleen had left the group together after Jason told them to stop arguing. Brooklyn said Rayleen had stomped off after Troy confronted her. And Jason said Rayleen got drunk and went out to puke. In both Brooklyn and Jason's retelling, Rayleen was the only one to leave the group before her body was found, which would mean there was another person on the island—someone outside the group—who'd done the killing.

In Carrie's version—at least the one she'd shared with me in her living room—Troy, Rayleen, Jason, Brooklyn, Katrina, and Trevor had all left the fire at one time or another before Rayleen was found dead, so any of them could have done it. Of course she'd change her story more than once as she'd discussed the events of the Massacre. I was trying to remember exactly what Troy had said to me, then turned the page to see what he'd told the officer who had interviewed him at the time of the murders.

Like Carrie, Troy said he'd left the group to argue with Rayleen and, like Carrie, he said she'd taken off and he'd returned to the group alone. The difference between his story and Carrie's was that Troy said everyone other than Rayleen was together when he returned and that they'd remained together until they found Rayleen's body. It struck me that in Troy's version of the story, he was the only one who could have killed Rayleen unless there really was another person on the island.

"This is really messed up," I commented. "I'm only through the first part, but the stories are already different enough that there's no way to make any sense of what might actually have happened. I'd say someone is lying, but it almost looks as if they were *all* lying."

"Keep reading."

The next part had to do with the actions of each individual after they found Rayleen's body. Brooklyn stated they'd organized search teams and gone looking for the killer. Troy said he didn't know what the others had done, but he'd taken off on his own. Jason said Troy took off and Josh and Trevor went after him while he returned to the fire with Carrie and Brooklyn. Carrie said Troy ran off into the storm, which fit Troy's story, but also that she and Joshua returned to the fire.

"It's like they were all trapped on deserted islands only they were in separate dimensions where some aspects of their experience were the same and others were different."

"I'll admit it's bizarre," Savage agreed.

"These interviews are all much too different even to be considered relevant."

"Which was the same conclusion the deputy who conducted the initial investigation determined. You can make yourself nuts trying to keep straight who said what and who agreed with whom, but in the end it doesn't matter because it's all gibberish."

"Where's the interview with Katrina?" I asked when I realized it wasn't in the packet.

"Katrina was almost catatonic when the kids returned from Waverly Island. She was unable to participate in an interview. After the deputy realized the interviews were basically useless anyway, he didn't follow up on trying to get her statement."

I found this also to be interesting. Normally, I would ask for copies of the interviews so we could map everything out on the white board back at the house, but the discrepancies were so significant that the only thing it made sense to take from what I'd just read was that there were significant discrepancies. The question was, *why* were the interviews so different? I'd read the case studies in sociology that talked about the way people who all had witnessed the same event described it differently, but this was ridiculous.

"Okay," I finally said, "gathering further witness statements will probably be a waste of time. Has anything else come to light about the original murders since the point at which the interviews were conducted?"

"No. We know Katrina moved away, but for the most part the other survivors settled back into their lives as if nothing had happened. I do remember there being some hoopla when the one-year anniversary of the Massacre came around, but really, other than a mention in the newspaper and some barroom conversation, it was like the whole thing never even occurred."

"If this was a movie we'd learn that the whole thing had been a dream in which everyone remembered the basic storyline yet their own version of it."

"That would make more sense than the reality. Someone killed those kids. Either there was someone else on the island or one of the survivors killed three of their friends."

"Two if Joshua really did pass out and drown."

"Two if Joshua passed out and drowned," Savage agreed. "However unlikely that is, I do suppose it's possible."

"We know Rayleen was stabbed. Was a murder weapon ever found?"

"No."

"What about blood on the hands or clothes of the survivors? If you stab someone thirteen times you're bound to get some blood on you."

"None of the kids had any blood on them that was obvious to the naked eye although most of them seemed to have brought a change in clothes to wear after swimming. It is possible out killer simply changed and ditched the bloody clothes. Because they were so traumatized, the deputy didn't take things further by examining them using luminol."

I took a minute to sort out my thoughts. It really did look as if the answer to the question of who'd killed three teenagers on a deserted island eleven years ago might never be answered, but perhaps we could make some progress regarding the question of what had happened to Katrina Pomeroy just a few days ago.

"I think Blackbeard might have seen Katrina jump, fall, or be pushed from the pier."

Deputy Savage didn't laugh or make a snide reply, so I assumed he was familiar with the extraordinary bird. Garrett had said it was Savage Blackbeard had called when he'd had his heart attack.

"Why do you think that?" Savage eventually asked.

"He got out on Friday when I was bringing in the groceries. When I was in town yesterday I spoke to both Sully and the clerk at the market, who informed me that Blackbeard had stopped by and chatted with them."

"What did Blackbeard say?"

"Sully said he was superchatty, but he wasn't paying that much attention, though he remembered him saying 'walk the plank' and 'Princess Anna.' Princess Anna is a character in a movie we watch together sometimes. She has long blond hair. Did Katrina have long blond hair?"

Deputy Savage took a photo out of his desk drawer and passed it to me. Sure enough, Katrina Pomeroy looked a lot like Princess Anna.

"So Blackbeard was trying to tell Sully that Princess Anna had walked the plank, which would look a lot like walking to the end of the pier and jumping or falling off."

"It seems that way," I confirmed.

"Did he see anything else? Another person?"

"I don't know. The only other thing he said was 'pickles and cream,' which doesn't make any sense no matter how I look at it. He might have seen someone wearing green, or maybe someone eating a pickle. It could even be some random comment that isn't important at all. I'm not sure it will do any good, but I'm thinking of taking

Blackbeard over to the pier. Maybe being there will jar a memory and he'll say something new."

"I guess it's worth a try. I'll come with you."

"Okay, great." I started to get up. "By the way, I need you to do something for me. When I was speaking to Troy he got an odd expression on his face just before he kicked me out."

"And you want me to arrest him for kicking you out?"

"No, of course not." I could see he was kidding, but still..."As soon as I left his office, he made a phone call. I want you to find out who he called. He used his office phone."

"Do you have a time?"

"It just so happens I do."

"Okay, then I'll put a trace on it. Anything else, as long as I'm doing your bidding?"

"Actually, yes, because you asked. Were the bodies of the three victims from the Massacre autopsied?"

"Yes."

"I don't suppose I could get a look at the reports?"

"Are you looking for something specific?"

"Not really," I admitted. "I just figured there could be something in the report detailing how they died that might lead us to who killed them."

"What sort of details?"

"I don't know. Anything. We might be able to determine the height of the person who killed Rayleen if we know the angle the knife that was used to kill her entered her body. The autopsy should also tell us if there were defensive wounds on Joshua's body or if he really did just pass out and drown. And then there's Trevor; someone must have pushed him onto that anchor. Maybe he struggled and there was evidence of bruising or other injuries. I won't know what I'm looking for until I see it."

"I'm sure the sheriff's department looked at all that eleven years ago."

"I'm sure they did, but it never hurts to put a fresh set of eyes on the problem."

Deputy Savage made a note. "Okay. I'll get the reports. I'll look at them, and as long as there isn't anything too confidential, we can look at them together. But again, what we find will be off the record."

Of course it will.

Chapter 9

I'm not sure if I believe in love at first sight, but I definitely believe in lust at first sight, which is exactly what was going on when Rick Savage met my absolutely stunning best friend, Victoria Vance. Victoria is not only a very successful author of steamy romantic suspense but she has the overall figure, hair, and skin to be cast in the lead role should Hollywood decide to make a movie of one of her books.

"Jilli!" Victoria greeted me with a hug. "I've missed you dreadfully."

"Me too." I hugged her in return.

"So," Victoria glanced at Savage, "introduce me to your friend."

"Victoria Vance, this is Deputy Savage."

"Rick," Savage said as he stuck out his hand.

"It's nice to meet you, Rick."

I couldn't help but notice the way *Rick* was almost drooling on himself as Victoria leaned in just a bit to return his handshake. Maybe it was her long dark hair, her big dark brown eyes framed with thick lashes, her perfect skin, or her jaw-dropping figure. Victoria had a way of demanding the attention of anyone she came into contact with, especially men.

"Rick is going to help me solve a murder," I informed her. Technically, Savage had never invited me to call him that, even though I'd known him a lot longer than Victoria had, but if she could call the deputy Rick so could I. "Do you want to come?"

"You know I do. Just let me change."

Victoria sashayed up the stairs in a red cashmere dress that was so form-fitting it left no doubt in anyone's mind as to the answer to the undergarments vs. no undergarment question. Her matching red pumps, which she wore on a regular basis so as to appear even taller than her five-foot-six, clickety-clacked on the hardwood flooring as she headed toward her room at the end of the hall.

"Your friend is..." Rick paused to clear his throat.

I just smiled. I'd known Vikki since we were kids, well before she'd developed her assets and learned how to use them. To men she was a sensuous goddess, but to me she was still the freckle-faced kid who'd worn braces for three years and had acne for another two.

"Gorgeous," I finished for Rick.

"I was going to say nice, but yeah, gorgeous works. You live together?"

I couldn't help myself; I offered him a suggestive grin that implied we not only lived together but we *lived* together.

"Oh, I'm sorry." Rick actually blushed. "I didn't mean to speak out of turn. It's really none of my business."

"Jilli, are you torturing this poor man?" Victoria asked as she returned in tight jeans, an even tighter sweater, and tennis shoes. She'd washed off most of her makeup and pulled her long hair back into a ponytail, instantly transforming her from sexy vixen to sexy girl next door.

"Why ever would I do that?" I replied innocently.

"Jilli and I have been friends since we were in pigtails and roller skates," Victoria said to Rick. "She can be a bit of an imp, but she's generally harmless. Are you married?"

"Married?"

"Legally bound to another."

"N-no."

"You sound uncertain."

Rick shook his head, as if trying to shake the wool from his brain. "No. I'm not married. Are you?"

"Painfully free. So about this murder..."

"We think Blackbeard may have seen something, so we're going to take him to the scene of the murder, suicide, or accident, we aren't sure which yet," I answered.

"Let me just grab a jacket. It's a bit nipply out."

I thought Savage was going to pass out when his eyes were automatically drawn to Vikki's chest.

"You okay there, bud?" I asked.

Savage cleared this throat. "Yeah. Terrific. I was just thinking about the case."

The case my ass. I grinned as Savage squirmed while we waited. I was having the best time.

Vikki got her jacket and we headed to the car. There was no way I was going to sit in the back of Savage's sheriff's car, so I'd convinced him that we'd take mine. We could have taken separate cars, but the way he and Vikki were undressing each other with their eyes, I doubted they'd be open to the suggestion. I'd seen other men react to Vikki in just this manner. A lot of other men. But somehow this seemed different. Perhaps a better word was *awkward*.

"So how was your trip?" I asked Vikki.

"Fabulous. Remember that editor from Forever Love Books I introduced you to at the Champagne Ball last year?"

"You mean Bill, or maybe it was Bob?"

"Brad."

"Yeah, that's right, Brad. What about him?"

"I ran into him this weekend and he said he was interested in publishing some of the backlist I regained rights to after the company I was with went under. I told him Harlequin has been after me to increase my presence with them and was hesitant to take on another obligation, but he said he might be able to sweeten the deal with a

Hallmark series if I would at least meet with his team."

"They want to turn your books into movies?"

"Not all of them, just a few. Isn't that fabulous?"

I glanced in the rearview mirror. Vikki had insisted on letting the deputy ride shotgun, so she sat behind me. "That really is wonderful, Vik. I hope it works out, though I've read your books. They don't seem like Hallmark material."

"We'll need to PG them up a bit, but that shouldn't be too much of a challenge."

"When are you planning to meet with Brad's people?" I asked.

"In two weeks. He's going to take me to Hawaii for a week before that so we can discuss a strategy. I guess we still need to convince his backers that making the books into movies is a good idea."

I couldn't help but notice Savage's face when Vikki announced she would be spending a romantic week in a tropical paradise with a man who wasn't him. Oh, yeah, the guy had it bad. This might be a personal record for Victoria. It usually took a few dates at least for a guy to fall head over heels for her particular brand of girl-next-door charm and raging-hot sexuality.

When we arrived at the pier I found a place to park, then removed Blackbeard from his travel carrier after making sure the tether was tied securely around my wrist and his leg. The last thing I wanted to do was chase a bird around Town trying to catch him if he got away. I didn't have a plan for our little excursion other than to take Blackbeard out onto the pier and wait to see his reaction to my questions.

"Walk the plank, walk the plank."

"Who walked the plank?" I asked.

"Princess Anna, Princess Anna."

"Did Princess Anna fall in the water?"

"Man overboard, man overboard."

"Was anyone with Princess Anna when she fell in the water?"

"Pickles and cream, pickles and cream."

"I don't understand what you mean by pickles and cream. Was someone eating a pickle?"

"Who's a good boy, who's a good boy?"

"You're a good boy and I'll give you a cracker in a minute, but first I want to see if you have anything else to tell me." I walked to the end of the pier and looked down into the water. The rocks beneath the surface were clearly visible. I know if I wanted to commit suicide I'd certainly find a more pleasant way of going about it. Somehow this whole thing wasn't making sense.

"Can you remember if someone hurt Princess Anna? Was there a bad person here when she walked the plank?"

Blackbeard tilted his head, making it appear as if he was giving serious consideration to my question.

"Did Princess Anna jump in?"

Blackbeard just looked at me.

"Was she pushed?"

"I don't think he knows anything," Victoria commented.

I glanced at Savage and shrugged.

"It was worth a try," Victoria comforted me. She glanced at Blackbeard. "How about it, big guy? Are you ready to go home?"

"Kiss and tell, kiss and tell."

Victoria laughed. "What does that mean? Do you have a secret, Blackbeard?"

******

I barely had time to get cleaned up for my *not a date* with Jack by the time we got home. Vikki mentioned she hadn't eaten all day and was starving and the next thing I knew, Savage was taking her out for a steak. And so it began: the dance of courtship, which, when Vikki was involved, most often ended with the man crying in his beer.

I stood in front of my closet, considering what to wear. On one hand, the main reason for the night out was a business meeting, so perhaps business casual was the choice of the day. Then again, this was Gull Island, where people tended to dress down no matter what the occasion, and I hated to show up looking all big city and unapproachable, so maybe jeans and a sweater? And then there was the dinner part of the evening. I'd made it clear to Jack that this was *not a date* and I'd just meet him at the restaurant, but that hadn't kept him from making a reservation at one of the nicer restaurants on the island. Would jeans be too casual?

The fact that I was standing in front of my mirror in indecision made me crazy. Before I gave up my old life and moved to Gull Island I used to be good at figuring out what to wear. Now I felt like a teenager on her first date.

Except this *wasn't a date*, I reminded myself. This was dinner before a meeting and nothing more. Deciding on soft suede slacks, a newish jacket, and my favorite boots, I changed as quickly as I could before running a brush through my hair, which really did need a trim, and heading into Town.

"I'm meeting Jackson Jones," I said to the host when I arrived at the restaurant.

"We've been expecting you. Please follow me."

I found my tension growing as I followed the man in the black jacket through the restaurant and into a private room. "We're eating in here?"

"The restaurant was booked, so I worked out a deal with the owner," Jack answered. "Besides, I have news, and eating in here will give us the privacy we need to chat."

I assumed his news pertained to the murder investigation, so I sat down in the chair Jack had pulled out for me.

"So what's your news?"

"Let's order first. Champagne?"

"We're going to a community meeting." I looked at the waiter, who was standing discreetly to one side. "I'll just have sweet tea."

"Coffee for me," Jack added.

"You do remember this isn't a date, right?" I reminded him. I was beginning to pick up a datelike vibe.

"You made that perfectly clear. Really, it was a draw between this and the Burger Bar, but I had a hotdog on a stick for lunch."

I couldn't help but chuckle. "You're a nut, you know that?"

"Yes. But a sexy nut. Like a macadamia."

"I was thinking peanut, but whatever floats your boat. So about your news...?"

Jack glanced at the waiter, who had just returned. We put in our order and waited for him to leave before he answered my question.

"I went online and did some research today. Most of what I found was totally irrelevant, but I did find a couple of things I consider to be interesting."

"Okay. Like what?"

"I spoke to the reporter who wrote the article for the *Gull Island News* eleven years ago. He's since left the area, but he agreed to tell me what he knew."

"So we're talking about the man who wrote the story we used to initially familiarize ourselves with the case?"

"Yes. Anyway, I mentioned that although the witness statements were very different, his article seemed to mirror Brooklyn Vanderbilt's statement. He said that while he'd initially planned to interview all the survivors he spoke to Brooklyn first, and somehow she convinced him to just run with the information she provided."

"Convinced him how?"

"All he would say about it was that Brooklyn was a *very* pretty girl who was *very* persuasive and made him an offer he couldn't refuse."

I rolled my eyes as I read between the lines. Sometimes men were pigs. The reporter was an adult, and at the time Brooklyn had still been a minor. The entire situation made me sick. "Okay, so that answers that question. Did the horny reporter provide any other relevant information?"

"He said he followed up on the report that the boat's radio hadn't been working on the day of the murders despite the fact that Jason's father had used it the day before and the radio was working fine."

"And...?"

"Someone had ripped out the wires."

"It had to have been one of the kids who disabled it," I realized. "If one of them did that it was most likely the same one who killed the others."

"That would be my guess."

I smiled at Jack. "This is relevant information. If our logic is correct it eliminates a random person who just happened to be on the island as the killer."

"I'm not sure I've ever seen you quite this animated before. Are you always this way when you're hunting down a story?"

"I am when I'm closing in on one."

The conversation paused when the waiter brought our food, which was fine because I needed a minute to digest the information Jack had just delivered. If the killer was one of the eight teens who went out on the boat that day, it meant the killer had to be Troy, Brooklyn, Jason, Carrie, or Katrina. If Katrina was pushed to her

118

death a few days ago that probably eliminated her as a suspect, but if she jumped to her death, that most likely pointed to her as the killer. Somehow, we needed to figure out which scenario was the correct one, and I thought I knew where to start.

Chapter 10

The crowd gathered to discuss the upcoming harvest festival was a lot bigger than I'd imagined it would be. This was, after all, a small community putting on a local event. I guess I'd thought there would be five or six people on the committee. Instead, I found a room full of volunteers when we entered the community center, all deep in discussion with those sitting closest to them regarding which food vendor to use and whether the weather would hold for the haunted hayride, which, as it turned out, was a sort of outdoor haunted house.

"Did you expect this many people?" I asked Jack.

"No. Although I suppose I'm not surprised. Everyone I've met since moving to Gull Island seems to be very much invested in their community."

"Let's grab a seat before they're gone. There are two next to the pregnant woman with the two children."

"You want to sit next to children? Who brings children to a community meeting anyway?"

"Maybe she couldn't get a babysitter." I took Jack's hand. "Come on before someone else grabs the chairs."

I led Jack through the room and sat down just as another group of people walked into the room. There was plenty of standing room, but I was exhausted and really didn't want to stand for the next two hours, so I was glad to have found the seats. I turned to the woman next to me. "Hi. I'm Jillian Hanford. This is my first meeting. I hope it's okay that we took these chairs."

"Brooke Johnson, and this is Stacy and Brian. I'm so happy to finally meet you."

"You know who I am?"

"Sure. It's not often that a famous reporter moves to our island." Brooke looked around me toward Jack. "And I'm happy to meet you as well, Mr. Jones."

"Jack is fine," he replied.

"The thing you need to know if you're going to sit at the front of the room is not to make eye contact with the volunteer coordinator unless you really want to take on whatever project she's trying to nail down volunteers for," Brooke warned us. "She's a real barracuda. If you meet her eye even for a second, she'll reel you in before you know you've been hooked."

"Thanks." I laughed. "I'll keep that in mind. I'm really surprised to see so many people have shown up."

"We're an active community. Most of the folks here won't actually volunteer for anything, but they like to be in the know."

Brooke turned her attention to the front as a woman in a pink cardigan took the podium.

"Thank you all for coming out," she began. "We have a lot to get through tonight. The festival is less than two weeks away, so the most important thing is to nail down the remainder of the volunteers needed to really pull this off, so without further ado, I'm going to ask Brooke to come to the front."

Brooke winked at me as I glanced at her with a look of surprise. "You're the barracuda?"

"In the flesh. But don't worry. I'll take it easy on you because you're new."

The meeting was both long and enlightening. After Brooke identified the volunteers she needed, the chairs for the larger events, like the hayride, took over. Each chairperson presented a detailed progress report and asked opinions about any decisions that still needed to be made. There was a positive energy in the room that helped me to feel both included and excited. It also turned out that Brooke's children were perfect angels and never made a peep during the entire meeting. I really did think I was going to enjoy being part of this pretty awesome community once I had a chance to get to know everyone.

Afterward Jack and I went out for pie and coffee. We'd both managed to get out of the meeting without any serious volunteer commitments, but I wasn't sure we'd be so lucky with the next event. Brooke hadn't exaggerated. She really was a barracuda who got what she set out to get, but she was bubbly and friendly, and it seemed as if everyone on the island adored her, which likely made doing her job that much easier.

"So what did you think of your first-ever community meeting?" I asked Jack.

"I enjoyed it very much. I honestly wasn't expecting to."

"If you weren't expecting to enjoy it why did you go in the first place?"

"I went because you said you were going and I figured the meeting would provide me with the opportunity to take you out on *not a date* and get to know you better."

"And do you feel you know me better now?"

He laughed. "Not at all. Why don't you tell me about yourself?"

"Okay, but if I do, you have to reciprocate."

"Deal."

I poured cream in my coffee before I began. "There really isn't much to tell. I'm thirty-eight and have spent the past fifteen years working on a variety of newspapers. I've never been married or had children, although I've traveled the world and have seen a lot of really fantastic things."

"But...?"

"But what?"

"There's always a *but*. I'm curious about what yours might be."

I shrugged. "There's no *but*. I worked hard, achieved my dreams, and have had a wonderful life."

"Okay, then what's your biggest regret?"

I flinched. "No regrets."

"Good try, but I saw the look of pain on your face when I asked, so again, what's your biggest regret?"

"I'm not sure that's something I want to talk about."

"I'm a good listener."

I hesitated.

"And I can keep a secret."

"Do you think discussing our biggest regrets is something we should be doing on our first date?" I asked.

"I thought this wasn't a date."

"It isn't. You know what I mean. Regrets are intensely personal."

Jack shrugged. "If you don't want to tell me that's fine, although I can probably guess."

"I doubt it."

"Okay if I try?"

No one other than a few people at the top knew what had really happened at the paper, so there was no way Jack could possibly know that my biggest regret had also been my biggest mistake.

"I'm going to assume no answer means yes," Jack continued when I didn't respond. "I'm going to guess that your biggest regret is that you never married or had children."

"What? That's crazy. I chose not to tie myself down and I don't regret it at all. My biggest regret has nothing to do with other people."

"Okay, then your biggest regret must have to do with your life as a reporter."

I looked away.

"Did you write something that ended up hurting someone?" Jack guessed.

"In a way, but not the way you're thinking."

Jack raised one eyebrow but didn't comment.

I took a deep breath and let it out. "If you must know, I didn't quit the newspaper. I was fired."

"Fired? Why?"

"Because I was stupid."

"I doubt that."

I looked Jack in the eye. "It's true. I was writing an article and was closing in on a deadline, although I still hadn't uncovered all the information I needed to really make the article stand out. At the very last minute, one of my sources—someone I'd used before and had always found very dependable—called me with the exact piece of information I needed to move my article from the back of the paper to the front page. My schedule was tight and I didn't have time to verify the tip, but my gut told me it was true, so I ran with it."

"Ouch." Jack scrunched up his face, making him look like he'd just taken a bite out of a lemon.

"After the story ran, the businessman I had targeted claimed my assertion was false. He accused me of lying. I hadn't been, but after I looked further I realized the information I'd received from my source was less than accurate. I'd been after this man for a long time; I was certain he was hiding environmental violations, but accusing him of what I knew he'd been doing when I didn't have the proof was the end of my career. He threatened to sue the paper if they didn't fire me."

"It sounds like maybe you were set up," Jack suggested.

"You think so?"

"Your source calls you at the last minute with the *exact* piece of information you think you need for your story, leaving you no time to verify it. Sounds hinky to me."

"You think my source lied?"

"I think maybe your source was fed false information. It was brilliant, really. You admitted you'd been after this particular businessman for environmental violations for a long time. Chances are you were getting close to the proof you needed to shut him down. The fact that someone dangled a big, juicy worm in front of you seems suspicious to me."

I hadn't considered the possibility that I'd intentionally been fed false information before, but it made sense. I had been getting close to proving that the chemical company in question was illegally disposing of waste, and the owner had gotten me off his back when I foolishly took the bait and printed his lies. *Geez, I was such an idiot.*

I looked at Jack. "You might be right about the false information, but it was still my fault. I was still the one who broke the first rule of journalism: Confirm the information you print before you print it. I should have known better, but I'd let myself become emotionally involved in the story and my overwhelming need to bring this man down caused me to act rashly, which led to my own demise." I looked Jack in the eye. "I left due to unspecified reasons and the newspaper agreed to keep the fact that I'd blown it to themselves. My reputation is important to me, and the way it worked out, most people who know me believe I really did leave the paper so I could move to Gull Island to help Garrett out. His call came at the perfect time. I'd really appreciate it if you would keep this to yourself."

Jack put his hand over mine. "I'm sorry it happened and I will absolutely keep your secret."

"Thank you. It feels good to have told someone. No one knows the truth. Not even Victoria."

"Any time you want to talk I'm here for you."

My eyes locked with Jack's. I'd found a sympathetic soul I could trust, and I didn't trust many people.

"Do you plan to look for another job in the industry?" Jack asked.

"Absolutely. I decided it was best to hide out for a bit, let all the speculation about what really happened die down, but I very much plan to reclaim my life at some point. I'm hoping this article will be just the thing I need to get people to take notice. If I can solve a decade-old murder I have a feeling job offers will start rolling in."

Jack smiled, although it didn't quite reach his eyes. "I wish you luck."

"Now it's your turn to tell me about your life," I reminded him.

"I'm forty-two and, like you, I've never been married or had children. I've had a lot of meaningless relationships but only one significant one that, in the end, didn't work out. I wrote my first best seller when I was nineteen and have written one every year since then."

"Biggest regret?"

"I guess I would have to say that was writing that first best seller."

Okay, I wasn't expecting that. "But why? It made you a success. It altered the course of your life."

"Exactly. It altered the course of my life. I wrote that book on a whim. I was a freshman in college working on a degree in journalism when my scholarship was pulled because the organization that provided it went under. I needed money and I needed it fast, so I decided to write a novel. I figured if I was lucky I'd sell a few copies and make enough to pay my rent and tuition."

"But you didn't sell a few; you sold a few million."

"Exactly. I dropped out of school, broke up with my girlfriend, moved to the city, got a fancy new car and an even fancier apartment, and started on novel number two. When that one was a hit as well there was no turning back."

"But you always wondered what might have been."

"Being a novelist was never my dream. Being a newspaper reporter, maybe someday owning a small newspaper, were the reasons I went to college in the first place."

"I get what you're saying, but you own a newspaper now, so I guess the moral of the story is that it's never too late."

"For the newspaper."

I frowned, and then it hit me. "But not the girl."

"We'd been together since we were sophomores in high school. I loved her. I planned to have a life with her, and I gave it all up on a whim. Instant success will do that to you. It will make you forget what's really important."

"Did you stay in touch?"

"No. I really hurt her, but she's married now, with three kids. She stayed in touch with my sister, who assures me that she's very happy. I'm glad things went her way. She deserved it."

I put my hand over Jack's as he had mine. "I'm sorry."

Jack squeezed my hand. "I guess, like you, the time for regret has passed. We both have the chance to start a new chapter in our lives. This time, perhaps we can learn from our mistakes and carve out a life that will remain regret-free."

I held up my coffee cup in a toast. "Here's hoping."

******

By the time I got home everyone had retreated to their own rooms. I made sure

Blackbeard was tucked in for the night, then headed upstairs as well. I knew I should be tired, but after my chat with Jack I felt restless, so I turned on my computer and settled in to do some research. This may seem odd, but doing research has always calmed my nerves. I wasn't sure what I was after, but after speaking to Jack I realized how valuable it was to have insight into a person's background.

On the day of the Friday the Thirteenth Massacre Jason Rogers had borrowed the boat from his father. He had two brothers and a sister and grew up in an intact household. His father liked to dabble in the stock market and had done very well. Jason had financial resources and the advantages many of his peers didn't until the stock market crashed. He hadn't paid as much attention to his education as he should have and so had been floundering financially ever since. His father had since passed and his mother and siblings had moved off the island.

Trevor Bailey also had grown up on the island. He'd lived with his mother and father and two younger sisters. He was an average student but a star athlete. After his death his family had moved to the West Coast.

Troy Wheeler was an only child who grew up with his single mom. He was small and somewhat awkward as a teen but seemed intelligent, especially when it came to numbers. After he graduated high school he got a job at the local bank and eventually worked his way up to manager after he completed his bachelor's degree online.

Joshua Vanderbilt grew up in Virginia. He lived with his mother and her husband. He didn't get along all that well with his stepdad, so he spent as much time on the island with Brooklyn's family as he could.

Brooklyn Vanderbilt also grew up on the island. She was raised by her father after her mother headed west to pursue a job in the entertainment industry. At the time of the Friday the Thirteenth Massacre she had just moved back to the island after having spent a year in Las Vegas with her mother.

Rayleen Oswald was from a family that had lived on Gull Island for two generations. As George had already learned, she was a seemingly popular student who used bullying to work her way to the top. She lived with her mother, father, and brother. She was the only one of the eight teens with a criminal record. She'd been arrested four times, all for assault and battery against other teens her age.

Carrie Quincy lived on the island with her aunt. I couldn't find any mention of what had happened to her parents. It seemed she was well liked in high school, although she wasn't on the A-list, like Brooklyn.

As I'd heard from both Carrie and George, Katrina Pomeroy was a loner who didn't appear to have any real friends. She'd grown up with her sister in an intact household but had suffered from bouts of depression from the time she hit puberty and been treated with antidepressants from that time. While the social media posts of the others were typical and unremarkable, I found I was drawn to Katrina's work. It was dark. It was angsty. It was brilliant. It seemed obvious to me after just a few minutes digging through her work that Katrina was not only a talented artist but a deeply emotional person as well.

It occurred to me that I should have Clara take a look at Katrina's work. I had a feeling the intuitive woman would see quite a lot in the poems and photographs Katrina had posted online for most of her life. Her work wasn't only dark, it was raw and personal, almost like a car accident. Some of it was so shocking that you knew you should look away, but the harder you tried to do it, the more you were drawn into the world Katrina created.

As I studied her work, I became more certain she could have been the killer. She seemed to feel things most kids her age didn't. Actions, cruel words and gestures most teenagers would brush off seemed to cut her to the depth of her being. And it wasn't only wrongs done to her that dug into her soul but wrongs committed against others, against the world as a whole. One short poem written just after the Friday the Thirteenth Massacre especially caught my eye.

I do not have a name
I do not have a face
You cannot hear me scream
Or witness my disgrace
But I see the things you do
From the shadows where I live
And one day soon I promise

My life for yours I'll give

I had no idea what it meant, though it seemed to indicate Katrina was planning to make a sacrifice for someone, although that person didn't seem worthy of it. Could she have committed suicide to protect someone else? Of course she'd written the poem eleven years before she died on the rocks at the foot of the pier. Chances were the poem and this recent event weren't related. Katrina had posted thousands of poems and photos over the years. I wasn't certain I'd find anything there, but I knew I would keep looking.

Chapter 11

Tuesday, October 17

I first met Clara Kline when she showed up on my doorstep shortly after I moved to Gull Island and announced she'd had a premonition that she was supposed to move to the resort, where she was destined to find her soul mate. Honestly, I wasn't sure what to make of the sixty-two-year-old woman dressed in a peasant blouse and matching skirt, but she seemed harmless enough, so I'd made a quick decision and let her in.

Clara was a unique, interesting person. She claimed to have psychic powers, which could account for why she walked around with her head in the clouds half the time, but she also often forgot where she left her keys or whether the garbage truck came by on Tuesdays or Thursdays. Shouldn't someone who claimed to know about the future be able to keep at least some of the details of the present straight in her mind?

"Have you seen the cat?" Clara asked me as she wandered into the kitchen, where I was making breakfast.

"We don't have a cat."

Clara looked confused. "No, I'm sure that's not right. I specifically remember a cat."

I glanced at Blackbeard, who was perched on his base in the corner of the communal area. "Blackbeard, do we have a cat?"

"Kill the cat, kill the cat."

"Oh my." Clara's hand shot to her mouth.

"Blackbeard is just kidding," I assured her after shooting a look of warning at the jokester parrot. "There is no cat. I've lived here for months now and have never once seen a cat. Maybe you had one before you arrived on the island."

Clara paused and looked around. "No," she said with confidence. "The cat wasn't from before. The cat is from now. I'm sure of it."

"Okay, if you say there's a cat I believe you, but it isn't here in this house, at least not right now, so how about some eggs?"

Clara didn't seem convinced but didn't argue. She sat down at the table and I placed a plate of eggs and toast in front of her."

"Coffee?"

"Two sugars," Clara answered.

I sat down at the table across from her and dug into my own plateful of eggs. I'd planned to show Clara the poems and photographs from Katrina's social media pages, but she seemed so dazed and confused I decided not to.

"Do you have plans today?" I asked conversationally.

"Once I find the cat I'm going to knit a scarf for the baby. It looks like he might not have a mother. He'll need a scarf."

"What baby, Clara? Are you talking about a friend's baby? Or a relative's?"

"No. Not a friend. Do we have honey? It's been a while since I've had any and it's one of my favorite ways to eat eggs."

Eggs and honey? "Uh, yeah, I think so. I'll look."

"Don't bother. The eggs are fine as they are." Clara pushed her plate across the table. She'd eaten only a single bite.

"Are you feeling okay?" I asked. "Breakfast is usually your favorite meal."

"I'm fine. I'm just worried about the cat. I think I'll continue my search of the house. I don't know where he could have gone off to."

I wondered if I should call a doctor. Clara was somewhat spacy on the best of days, but today she seemed downright crazy. Could she have had a stroke?

"Have you seen your doctor recently?" I asked.

"No. Not since last summer."

"Do you think maybe we should call him?"

"Why ever would I call him? Do you think he knows what happened to the cat?"

"I think he might. I'll call him to ask."

I called Clara's doctor as soon as she headed upstairs and was out of earshot. He agreed it might be best to check things out, so I made an appointment to bring her in later that morning. I hadn't known Clara long, but I'd grown fond of her. I really hoped she was going to be okay. This wasn't the first time I'd caught her talking gibberish, so maybe the whole drama surrounding the cat was just Clara being Clara and not a medical condition.

I was about to put the kitchen in order when my phone rang. It was Deputy Savage.

"Deputy," I greeted him.

"I heard back from the phone company. Troy Wheeler called a business number after you left his office the other day."

"What business?"

"Conway Marine. It's a supply store located on a neighboring island. I know Troy has a boat. If you ask me, the phone call wasn't in any way related to the conversation the two of you were having."

"Are any of the Massacre survivors related to Conway Marine in any way? Have any of them worked there or do any of them have siblings, friends, or parents who work there?"

"Not that I know offhand, although I suppose it's possible."

"Do we know who in the company he called?"

"No. I've been pondering the value of calling and trying to find out who Troy spoke to, but we

138

don't have a reason to suspect him of doing anything wrong. It might seem like harassment, and he's the bank manager and an island council member. I don't think it's wise to start snooping around in his private business when we have absolutely no reason to do so."

I had to admit the deputy had a point. If we checked out Conway Marine and it got back to Troy that we were looking into his phone records for absolutely no reason it wouldn't go over well.

"I guess the phone call could just have been a phone call," I said. "While I have you on the line, did you ever look at Katrina Pomeroy's photography and poetry? I mean really *look* at it?"

"I've heard it's dark and disturbing, but no, I haven't taken the time to sit down and go through it."

"Maybe you should. I read some of her poetry last night and the entire time I had this nagging feeling she was trying to tell me something. Not me specifically because we never met, but the *me* of the bigger *we*."

"Huh?"

"Just take a look at it. I was going to show it to Clara, but she's acting weird. So weird that I'm going to take her to the doctor today. Oh, did you get the autopsy reports?"

"I did."

"And did anything jump out as being important?"

"I've only had a chance to glance at them, but not really."

"Maybe I'll stop by your office later. I have some other things I want to discuss with you. I'll call you after I get back from the doctor."

"Did Victoria get home okay?"

"Home? Home from where?"

My question was met with silence.

"She stayed over at your place last night," I realized.

"For a while. When I woke up she was gone. I called her, but she didn't pick up. I'm not being one of those clingy guys, I promise. I just wanted to make sure she made it home safely."

I closed my eyes and let out a groan. I didn't need this man distracted. I needed him focused on this case. "I haven't seen Victoria, but she usually sleeps until at least one, so I imagine she's still in bed. I'll poke my head into her room just to make sure that's where she is. I need to warn you, though, that Victoria tends to chew men up and spit them out. Don't get emotionally involved with her. You'll only end up getting hurt."

"Your concern is duly noted."

******

The doctors' offices on Gull Island were all located in a medical complex that also provided a small urgent care center. Clara had only been to the doctor on Gull Island once shortly after she arrived, and that was so she could have her prescriptions refilled. I had no idea if this doctor had the skillset necessary to check for a stroke or some other medical reason for her behavior, but unless I took her to Charleston the choices were limited.

"Clara doesn't show any of the typical symptoms of having suffered a stroke," the doctor informed me. "But she does appear to be confused. I'm going to recommend additional testing that will need to be done in a larger facility. Here's a list." He handed me the names of facilities that could do the tests, complete with phone numbers. "I don't think there's any urgency at this point, but here's a list of symptoms to watch for. Once she's had the tests bring her back and we'll go over the results."

I thanked the doctor and took Clara's arm to lead her out to the car. There was a longhaired black cat sitting on the grass next to the passenger door.

"There you are, you silly cat. I wondered where you'd gone off to."

"Is this the cat you were talking about?"

"Yes. Agatha. I knew she was supposed to arrive today and I was so sad when I couldn't find her."

Okay, now what was I supposed to do? Clara was holding Agatha, who looked quite content while she waited for me to open the car door. I didn't want to tell her she couldn't bring the cat home with her, though I didn't want to aid and abet her stealing the cat either.

"I need to run back inside." I opened the passenger door for them. "You and Agatha can wait here. I'll just be a minute."

I hurried back into the medical complex and up to the reception desk. "Excuse me; this is going to seem odd, but do you happen to know if anyone in the area has a longhaired black cat?"

"Not that I know of," the dark-haired girl answered. "Why do you ask?"

"There was a cat out by my car. The woman I brought in seems to think the cat belongs to her, but I've never seen it before in my life. I hate to leave the cat behind, but I also don't want to steal someone's cat if she isn't a stray. If I leave my number will you let me know if someone comes around looking for her?"

"Sure. You might want to post a notice in the paper as well."

"Good idea." I jotted down my cell number, then headed back to my car, where Clara was sitting talking to the cat.

"Are we all set?" Clara asked.

"All set. Do you need to go anywhere else as long as we're out?"

"No. I should get home. Now that Agatha has been found I should get started on that scarf. It won't be long before the baby arrives."

******

I dropped Clara and Agatha at home, reminding Clara that she needed to keep Blackbird in his cage while the cat was around, then headed back into Town. My goals for the day were twofold. I wanted to stop by Betty Boop's and get the trim I'd discussed with the hairdresser mayor and I wanted to visit the elementary school to see if I could orchestrate things so I'd run into Brooklyn Vanderbilt. The school didn't get out until three, so I started with Betty Boop's.

Entering the salon was like taking a step back in time. It was bright and colorful and reminded me of a fifties diner. There were three hairdressers on duty, including Betty Sue Bell, and all of them had hair as big as Betty Sue's personality. When I got a look at the woman who would be doing the trimming I almost turned around and ran in the opposite direction.

"I'm so glad you made it in," Betty Sue said before I could slip out. "This here is Ellie May and this is Wanda Rhea. Go ahead and have a seat and one of us will be right with you."

I did as Betty Sue directed and took a seat next to two women who were reading magazines. The nostalgic atmosphere of the place did bring back warm memories of my grandmother's house, which I'd visited on many occasions when I was young. While my mother is and was a flamboyant diva who was interested only in herself, I remember my grandmother as being a warm, loving person who made me cinnamon toast in the broiler and served every meal on matching china and place mats.

As I sat there, it occurred to me I should call my mother. It had been several months since I'd moved to the island and I'd never even told her that I'd reconnected with my father and met a half brother I never knew I had.

"You lookin' for a color or just a trim?" the woman with pink hair who I remembered was Wanda Rhea asked.

"Just a trim."

"Layers?"

Did I dare let this woman loose with a scissors? "No. Just a trim. I can come back another time if you're busy."

"No worries, suga. We can fit you in. How's that brother of yours doin'?"

"Better."

When the woman Wanda Rhea had been working on got up to leave I was relieved to see her hair was nicely shaped and artfully dried to frame her face. Wanda Rhea indicated that I should take a seat in her chair while she headed to the cash register to take payment from the client she'd just finished with.

"I saw you at the town meeting last night sitting next to Brooke," Ellie May said.

"Betty Sue invited me to volunteer to work on the harvest festival. I'm looking forward to it. Being new to the island, I'm anxious to meet the people who live here."

"Brooke told me that you're a journalist."

"I used to work for a newspaper, but for the time being I just do freelance writing."

"Brooke said you're writing about those kids who died."

I was surprised Brooke knew that; I hadn't mentioned it to her, but it was a small island and she seemed to be a popular woman who knew a lot of people. I suppose anyone—Carrie, Gertie, or even Troy—could have mentioned it to her. "Yes, I'm working on an article about the Friday the Thirteenth Massacre as a sidebar to Katrina Pomeroy's death."

"That young'un was never quite right," Wanda Rhea joined in after returning to us. "There are some who say she carried the mark of the devil."

"The devil?" I asked.

"She had a dark side. If you weren't careful you could lose yourself in her black eyes," Wanda Rhea shared. "Folks on the island were sorry about what happened to those kids but real glad when her family moved away."

I thought back to the photos I'd seen of Katrina. She had dark eyes that provided a significant contrast to her blond hair and pale skin, but I wouldn't say they were black.

"Do any of you know if Katrina ever visited the island after she moved away before last week?"

Wanda Rhea and Ellie May agreed they hadn't seen or heard from her.

"If you're really interested you might want to speak to Jimmy Breelin," Betty Sue suggested.

"Were they friends?"

"Jimmy and Katrina were best friends when they were kids. Everyone knew Jimmy was sweet on her. I wouldn't be surprised if he made an effort to keep in touch."

Wanda wrapped a pink cape around my shoulders. "Do you know where I can find Jimmy?" I asked.

"Works over at the hardware store," Betty Sue provided.

"Let's get you shampooed," Wanda Rhea said. "Then we'll see what we can do to put some life back in your hair."

"Just a trim," I reminded her. The last thing I wanted to do was deal with the agony of growing out a bad cut.

"Don't worry, suga. Wanda will fix you up just right."

As it turned out, Wanda did an excellent job. In fact, my hair had never looked better. I thanked her, left her a big tip, and headed out to my car. I still had some time before school let out for the day, so I decided to track down the one lead I had: Jimmy Breelin. The hardware store was just down the street, so if luck was on my side, I could talk to Jimmy and then catch up with Savage.

Chapter 12

Jimmy Breelin was as light and breezy as my new haircut. His smile was almost as wide as his face and his demeanor so jolly that I swear he bounced when he walked. If he'd been best friends with Katrina his lightness must have contrasted with her darkness to a remarkable degree.

"Well, hey there, darling, what can I do for you today?" he greeted me.

His smile was so wide and his teeth so big that he reminded me of a happy clown.

"My name is Jillian Hanford," I introduced myself. "I'm a journalist and I hoped to speak to you about Katrina Pomeroy."

Jimmy's smile faded just a bit. "I talked to Carrie. She told me you were looking in to things. She also said you think Katrina killed herself, but she wouldn't."

"Did you keep in touch with her after she moved off the island?"

"After a bit."

Jimmy and I were standing in one of the hardware store aisles, which admittedly wasn't the best location for this conversation. "Is there somewhere we could talk? Somewhere a bit more private?"

"There's an office in the back. Just let me tell someone what I'm doing."

Jimmy informed the other clerk that he was taking a break and then led me to a small office at the back of the store. He indicated I should take a seat on one side of the desk while he sat down on the other. I could see he was nervous, and to be honest, I was surprised he'd agreed to speak to me.

"What do you want to know?" Jimmy asked.

"I understand you and Katrina were friends."

"Yes, we were friends. Good friends."

"Based on what I know of Katrina's personality, it appears the two of you were very different."

"Not in the ways that count."

"What do you mean by that?"

"Sure, Katrina was dark and moody and I've been accused on more than one occasion of being nauseatingly perky, but that's *how* we are, not *who* we are."

I paused as I considered the man before me. I guess I understood what he was trying to say. We live a life on the inside that's reflected on the outside, but how we choose to interact with people isn't necessarily our true self. "Can you tell me what you mean by that?"

"Katrina seemed dark and moody. She had a melancholy personality that led others to see her as depressed. On the surface it appeared she lived a solitary life removed from those she shared her space with, but in truth, Katrina was an emotionally gifted individual who felt deeply and loved with all her heart. The problem was that she didn't always know how to communicate what she was feeling or make the best choices when it came to giving her love away."

"Loved with all her heart?"

"The only reason she even agreed to go on the boat trip that day was to spend time with the person who had won her heart."

"She was in love with one of the guys?"

"Not one of the guys; one of the girls."

I frowned. "Which one?"

"Brooklyn. Not that Katrina ever had a chance with Brooklyn, who is straight, but that didn't stop Katrina from pining over her. Personally, I didn't understand the attraction, and it bothered me that Katrina was so deeply committed to someone who barely knew she was alive. It was truly sad, and I'll admit Katrina's infatuation with Brooklyn put a strain on our friendship. We stopped hanging out and Katrina started spending time with Carrie, who gave her access to that crowd."

"Did Carrie know about Katrina's feelings for Brooklyn?"

"I don't think so."

"Okay, so at the time of the killings you weren't friends with Katrina?"

Jimmy bowed his head. His perkiness had all but disappeared. "We were estranged friends, but I knew she'd be back. The reality is that one can only live a lie for so long before the truth makes its way through. I knew once Katrina's truth was revealed she'd come running back to me."

"And did you reconnect with Katrina after the murders?"

"Not at first, but then she called me from out of the blue a year or so ago. She was getting ready to move to Charleston, and it seemed like she was in a good place, so I met her in the city and we caught up. We stayed in touch after that."

"Did you know she was coming to Gull Island last week?"

Jimmy shook his head. "No. She never said a word about it."

"Do you know why she might have been here?"

Jimmy sat back in his chair with a look of contemplation on his face. I waited quietly in the dusty room that smelled of cigarettes and urine, which weren't typical scents associated with a hardware store. I glanced at the door to my side, which was open and revealed a filthy bathroom. I wrinkled my nose against the stench and hoped Jimmy would resume the conversation and distract me from the smell of the place.

"Honestly," Jimmy finally spoke, "I have no idea why she would have come back to the island. Brooklyn is married now, so Katrina had to know she wouldn't have a shot with her, and I know the events on Waverly Island eleven years ago truly traumatized her. Coming back here would be like taking a trip into her nightmares for Katrina. It wouldn't be a decision she took lightly, so I assume she had a really good reason."

"Brooklyn is married now," I repeated, something I'd known from Charles's report.

"Yes. That's what I just said."

"And she married Flip Johnson?"

"Yes. They have two children. Cute little things."

I looked directly at Jimmy. "Are Brooklyn Vanderbilt and Brooke Johnson the same person?"

"Yes. Like I said, Brooklyn is married now."

Pickles and cream.

"I have to go."

I drove as fast as I could to the sheriff's office. If Katrina was murdered I knew who the killer was.

******

"Oh good, you're here," I said as I rushed into Savage's office, closing the door behind me. "I know who was with Katrina when she fell, jumped, or was pushed from the pier."

"Who?"

"Brooklyn Vanderbilt, who I guess is now Brooke Johnson." I rushed forward and sat down across from him. "When I asked Blackbeard who was with Princess Anna on the pier he said 'pickles and cream.' Brooke Johnson is pregnant."

Deputy Savage looked confused.

"Don't you get it? Blackbeard saw a pregnant woman with Katrina and remembered that pregnant women have cravings for pickles and ice cream."

Savage didn't seem convinced. "That's quite a stretch. How would Blackbeard even know about the pickles and ice cream thing?"

"Garrett used to watch a lot of TV with Blackbeard. He must have picked it up somewhere."

"Even if that's true, the leap from pickles and cream to Brooke Johnson is huge."

"There's more. I just spoke to Jimmy Breelin. He told me that back in high school Katrina was in love with Brooklyn."

"Brooklyn is gay?"

"No, but Katrina is—or was."

Savage let out a breath that sounded more like a groan. "Are you saying Brooke Johnson killed Katrina? Why would she do that? She's married, with two great kids and a third on the way. Even if Katrina was in love with her and Brooke somehow found out, I don't see her killing the woman over such a thing."

I grabbed the poem I'd jotted down from my backpack and pushed it across the desk. "Look at this. Katrina wrote it."

I do not have a name
I do not have a face
You cannot hear me scream

Or witness my disgrace
But I see the things you do
From the shadows where I live
And one day soon I promise
My life for yours I'll give

Savage read it and then looked up at me.

"What if Brooklyn killed those kids on the island?" I asked. "What if Katrina somehow knew it? What if Katrina had been living with that secret for eleven years? What if it all became too much, so she got in touch with Brooke and asked her to meet her? What if she confronted Brooke and Brooke pushed Katrina to her death?"

"That's a lot of what-ifs."

"It is," I admitted, "and I have no idea how to prove it, even if it's true."

"Based on the poem, it looks as if Katrina is saying she's going to sacrifice herself for someone. That doesn't sound like a murder. That sounds like a suicide."

"It does," I agreed. "But what if the poem relates to the past as well as portends the future?"

"Come again?"

"In the beginning Katrina writes about being nameless and faceless. Based on what I've just learned, Katrina was in love with Brooklyn, who barely knew she was alive. In the middle we learn Katrina knows something. She says she sees what she does. What if she saw Brooklyn kill those kids? And in the end, the part about giving her life for hers—maybe she knew that one day

153

she would die at Brooklyn's hands. Maybe she even jumped. She could have if she felt doing so would somehow help Brooklyn."

Savage rubbed his hands across his face. The poor man looked completely overwhelmed. He'd probably known sweet, beautiful Brooke her entire life. I'd brought him a lot to digest.

"Okay," he finally said. "Say this is all true. Say Katrina agreed to go on the sailing trip to be close to Brooklyn, who she loved from afar. And say she followed Brooklyn out into the storm, where she witnessed her killing three people. She doesn't know how to deal with it and has a mental breakdown. She moves away and gets therapy and eventually gets her life back on track. Maybe she even knows it's her destiny to die for Brooklyn. Why?"

"Why what?"

"Why everything? Why would she come to Gull Island if she knew she was going to die?"

I paused. "I don't know. Maybe there's a piece to this puzzle we're missing."

"Maybe. And maybe the whole thing is just a convenient story that has no basis in reality. I'm not saying you haven't brought up some good points, but there's no way I'm going to confront Brooke in any way until we have proof."

Acting without proof had cost me a lot already. "Okay. You're right. So what now?"

"We just keep looking in to it. We'll put this whole thing with Brooke on a shelf and see if we find anything that supports or negates it."

"All right. That makes sense."

"And don't go around telling everyone what you suspect. Brooke is a popular teacher and member of the community. Trust me when I say it won't go well for you here if it gets out that you suspect her of murder."

"I'll tell Jack, but no one else. Jack can help. He has a way of seeing what others don't."

"Okay, you can tell Jack, but that's it. If you meet with your writers' group you need to lead them to believe you still don't know what pickles and cream might mean."

"Okay. For now."

Savage shook his head. "Wow. Brooke Johnson. I really hope to God you're wrong."

"Yeah." I remembered the sweet, friendly woman I'd met the night before. "Me too. By the way, the writers are meeting tonight to discuss the case. You're welcome to join us if you'd like."

"I don't know that I should be meeting with a group of civilians to discuss an open investigation."

I shrugged. "Suit yourself. Victoria will be there."

I couldn't help but notice the interest in his eyes as he mumbled something about letting me know later. I felt bad that the guy was heading for heartbreak. I was really starting to like him.

"So you spoke to her?"

"No," I said. "I was going to check on her before I left the house, but I forgot. I'll have her call you when I get home. Like I said, Vikki likes to sleep late, but she should be awake by the time I get there."

Savage averted his gaze. "That's okay. There's no need to bother her. I just wanted to make sure she was okay. I'll text you later to let you know about tonight."

Chapter 13

Although the thought of Brooke as the killer made me physically nauseous, there wasn't a lot I could do to prove or disprove my theory at the moment so I headed home. I was still somewhat worried about Clara, even though she was as happy as could be since she'd found the cat she'd been looking for. I wanted to make sure her symptoms hadn't worsened. While it wasn't unusual for Clara to walk around with her head in the clouds, this morning's behavior had seemed excessive. I hoped I could convince her to have the tests her doctor had recommended, though she'd refused to talk about them on our drive back to the house.

"Anyone home?" I called as I hung up my light jacket and backpack.

"Outside on the deck," Clara answered.

I wandered through the living area toward the back door. It was a beautiful, sunny day and sipping a cola while sitting in the sun seemed like a wonderful idea. When I arrived on the deck I found Clara sitting on a lounge chair knitting, with the cat she'd found curled up next to her. "Where's everyone else?"

"Charles is getting settled into his new cabin, Alex and Brit headed out to grab a bite to eat, and I haven't seen Victoria all day."

I frowned. "I'm going to grab a cola; would you like one?"

"Sweet tea if we have it."

"I think there's still some left. I'll check. It really is a lovely day."

"Yes, it is, although I'm afraid the sunshine won't last long. There's another storm coming."

"Really? I hadn't heard." I looked up into the sunny sky. Not a cloud anywhere. Clara really was off her game. I headed inside to grab the drinks but decided to check on Victoria first. It was totally like her to sleep late, but not this late. I knocked on her door, but there was no answer, so I tried the knob, which turned. I opened the door a crack to find a deserted room. There was no sign the bed had been slept in. In fact, the dress she'd changed out of the previous day was still laid out across the bedspread. At this point I was more curious as to where she'd gone off to than concerned, so I headed to the kitchen. I was halfway down the stairs when I remembered I'd left Blackbeard in his cage, a necessary precaution now that we had a cat in the house. I detoured to the sunroom, where I'd last seen him resting, and asked him if he'd like to go out onto the deck.

"Kill the cat, kill the cat."

"Yes, I understand you aren't fond of the cat, but Clara seems very happy to have her, so you're going to have to get used to her." I opened the door of the cage and attached the tether to Blackbeard's leg.

"I think I might have figured out what you meant by pickles and cream," I said to the bird as we headed toward the deck. "The woman with Princess Anna. Was she pregnant?"

Blackbeard looked at me but didn't reply.

"Did she have a big belly?" I asked as I transferred him to his perch.

Still he didn't reply.

I picked up a blanket Clara had brought out but set aside and tucked it up under my shirt.

"Pickles and cream, pickles and cream."

"That's what I thought," I said and set the blanket back on the chair. I turned to Clara. "I'm going to get our drinks. Be sure to watch the cat around the bird."

"Of course, dear. We wouldn't want the bird to hurt Agatha."

That wasn't what I meant, but whatever. As long as she kept the two animals away from each other it should be fine. When I returned to the deck I asked Clara about the scarf she was working on.

"It's for the baby."

"The one who might be without a mother?" I asked.

"Yes. It's all so uncertain now, but there's a possibility he won't have his mother to nurture him as babies should. The scarf will comfort him."

I had to admit I was starting to become concerned about this baby. Clara seemed to be extra loopy today, but she did occasionally have verifiable visions. Was there a baby in danger?

"Do you know who the baby is?"

"His name is Peter."

"Do you know his last name or perhaps his mother's name?"

Clara thought about it. "No. I'm not picking up the mother, just the baby."

"Is he okay?"

"For now."

Well, that was something. I'd need to mention Clara's baby to the others. Maybe someone would know something about him that I didn't.

"I was wondering if we could chat about your gift," I began.

"The scarf?"

"No, not that gift. I wanted to ask you about your ability to see into the future. To understand what others can't."

Clara set her knitting aside. "Okay. What would you like to know?"

"Do you think it's possible for a person such as yourself to look in to the future and see your own death?"

Clara paused before answering. "I suppose one could have a vision that would allow them to witness their own death. Why do you ask?"

I handed Clara Katrina's poem. "It seems to me," I began, "that the person who wrote this

160

poem knew how and when she was going to die when she wrote the poem. If she did, could she have done something to change what was going to happen?"

"Visions are like dreams. They don't have a substance or texture you can touch and manipulate. There is the possibility that the poet had a vision that she would die and that the individual she wrote the poem for would be involved in some way, but it is more likely that the phrase *my life for yours I'll give* is a metaphor for something other than physical death."

"Like what?"

"It's hard to know what was in the poet's heart, but *my life for yours* could mean she was going to be faced with the choice to give up something that was important to her, maybe even life-defining, for the other person. It's like when you gave up the life you had built in New York to come to Gull Island to protect the land that is so very important to Garrett. You gave something that was important to you so Garrett could have something that was important to him."

"I didn't really give up my life," I backpedaled. I was beginning to feel guilty that everyone thought I'd made this huge sacrifice when really, Garrett's offer had saved me from the mess I'd made of my own life. "But the poem...could it be taken literally? Could someone know ahead of time that it was their destiny to give up their life for someone else?"

"I suppose."

"And if that were true could they have taken measures to change things?"

Clara paused before answering. "Maybe. Some believe the future is fluid and without form, that you can alter what is to be by making a change in the present. Others believe the future is woven on predestined fabric that can be sensed but not changed."

"Which do you believe?"

Clara looked directly into my eyes. "I'm not sure. My experience has been that the future is set, and while it can be perceived, it cannot be altered. My hope, however, is that our ability to experience the future serves as a vehicle for us to change that which must be changed."

"Have you ever seen something you wished you hadn't seen?"

Clara glanced down at her lap. She gave the cat a scratch behind the ears and then resumed her knitting. It was obvious I had asked a question she was unable or unwilling to answer.

I finished my soda and took Blackbeard back into the house. I put him in his cage and then headed upstairs to freshen up. I'd just run a brush through my hair when I received a text.

If you continue to dig into the past, the life sacrificed may not be the last.

I frowned. First the note on my car, now this text. It seemed clear to me that I was getting close to something. I called Savage and told him about the text. He asked me to stop by so we could try to trace the source of the message. I supposed that while I was there it might be a good idea to mention that it looked as if Victoria

162

hadn't come home the previous evening after all. I hated to worry him, but Victoria hadn't texted me back either, which wasn't like her at all.

******

As it turned out, the text had been sent from a burner phone, so there was no way to identify who had initiated it. The fact that I had received both a threatening note and a threatening text seemed to bother Savage more than he wanted to let on. I'm pretty good about reading body language and facial expressions and I could see he was deeply concerned. When I told him that Victoria hadn't come home I thought he was going to pop an artery.

"Is it like her to simply disappear this way?" Savage asked.

"No. Not at all. She always returns my calls and texts, and if she's going to be in an area without service she lets me know ahead of time so I won't worry about her. You don't think her disappearance and the text are related, do you?" I couldn't get the words *the life sacrificed may not be the last* out of my mind.

"I hope not."

Something occurred to me. "Did Victoria have her car last night?"

"No. I picked her up for our date."

"Then how did she leave in the middle of the night?"

"I guess I just assumed she either took a taxi or called a friend for a ride."

"I'm probably the friend she would have called and I didn't hear from her, so she must have taken a taxi. There can't be that many taxi companies on the island. Maybe you should call around to find out who picked her up."

"There are only two companies. I'll call them both."

"I'll call Brit and Alex while you do that. I doubt she would have called either of them for a ride, but I supposed she might have if I hadn't picked up my cell."

Brit and Alex confirmed what I already knew: neither had been called for a ride and neither had spoken to Victoria since she'd returned from her trip.

"Any luck?" I asked after Deputy Savage completed his own calls.

"Neither company had a pickup at my address on their books, but the second company I called told me that a woman had called for a pickup from an address just a block from my house at two-thirty a.m. When the driver arrived she wasn't there. The house was deserted."

My heart sank. "So if Vikki didn't take a taxi where is she?"

"I don't know." Savage ran his hand through his full head of hair. "We can try pinging her phone. Do you have the number?"

"Yeah." I wrote it down and handed it to him. He made the call and we waited for a reply.

"It has to be Brooke," I insisted. "I know we don't have proof, but we have a good theory, and when I was home earlier I put a blanket under my shirt to look pregnant and Blackbeard immediately said 'pickles and cream.' Brooke must have killed Katrina, and now she's going to kill Victoria and it will be all my fault."

"We don't know Brooke killed Katrina," Savage reminded me. "We don't even know she was with Katrina when she died. There are other pregnant women on the island."

"Maybe, but I doubt there are other pregnant women who wanted to keep Katrina from sharing what she knew."

"We don't know Katrina knew anything or that Brooke did anything. I want to find Victoria as badly as you do, but we can't go off half-cocked."

Savage's phone rang. "Hey, what did you find?" he asked. "Okay thanks." He hung up and looked at me. "The phone is turned off."

"What are we going to do now?"

"I'm not sure," he admitted. "It's too early to file a missing persons report. For all we know, she has another guy on the island who picked her up and took her over to his place."

Savage had a point. Victoria did have men on the island she sometimes *dated* and I could totally see her calling one of them to come get her, but that didn't explain why she'd turned off her phone, which she *never* did, and failed to return my calls, which she *always* did.

"If Brooke is the bad guy—and I'm not saying she is—and she has Victoria for whatever reason, maybe we can find out where she's taken her. Brooke will be in class for another half hour. We can follow her when she leaves the school to see where she goes," Savage suggested.

"That might be a good idea. Should we confirm she's even at the school? She could have called in sick."

"I'll call over to find out."

I got up and paced around the office while Savage made the call. I'd never forgive myself if something happened to Victoria. I did wonder, though, why of all the people in my life Victoria was taken. That didn't make sense. If someone had kidnapped her, how would they have known she was at Savage's in the first place? And even if this person had followed the couple to his home, how had they known when to pick Victoria up?

"She's in class," Savage informed me, "which will be over in thirty minutes. She'll be off work for the day shortly after that. We should get in place."

"We'll take my car. Trying to discreetly follow someone in a sheriff's vehicle would probably be impossible."

"Okay, but I'll drive," Savage insisted. "And we won't confront her. If we follow her to a location we think might be a hiding place I'll call for backup and you'll wait in the car."

"I'll do whatever you say, but if we find Victoria, getting her to safety takes precedence over anything else."

Sitting in my car in front of an elementary school with dozens of parents waiting to pick up their little darlings was a nerve-racking experience. For one thing, the area directly surrounding the school was total chaos, and for another, the waiting to find out if Victoria was dead or alive was killing me.

"How much longer?" I wondered.

"Classes will let out in about five minutes. I expect we'll see Brooke come out from the building twenty to thirty minutes after that."

"That long?"

Savage shrugged. "Maybe. I'm not aware of her after-school routine, but it would seem she would need to straighten up, turn in attendance, that sort of thing."

I tried calling Victoria again while we waited, but it went straight to voice mail. I was so nervous I felt like I was going to jump out of my skin. The waiting was torture.

"Clara thinks the line *my life for yours I'll give* from Katrina's poem might not have been meant literally," I said, mostly to fill the time. "She thinks it could mean Katrina was planning to give up something that was important to her to be close to Brooklyn. Of course she wrote the poem eleven years ago, so even if that was her plan at the time she never followed through on it."

"So you don't think Brooklyn killed Katrina?" Savage asked.

"No, I totally think Brooklyn killed Katrina; I'm just not sure Katrina knew what was going to happen, as I originally imagined. Oh look, here come the kids."

The next fifteen minutes we found ourselves in the middle of mass chaos as kids ran in front of cars that were jockeying into position in front of the school to pick up the little monsters that seemed to be everywhere all at once. "This is crazy."

"Yeah," Savage agreed. "It does seem the school ought to develop a better after-school procedure. I'll have a chat with the principal."

The kids finally all cleared out and we just needed to wait another ten minutes before the teachers began to emerge from the building.

"Look. There she is." I pointed to a woman in a sunny yellow maternity top.

Savage started the car and pulled in behind her, making sure not to get so close as to be spotted. We followed Brooke to a house Savage informed me wasn't her own. We waited while she got out and went inside. When she returned she had her two children with her.

"This must be her day-care provider's home," I said, disappointment in my voice. There was no way she was going to lead us to someone she'd kidnapped with her kids in tow. Just to be sure, we followed her to her home, where she went inside and didn't come out.

"It's possible Brooke doesn't have Victoria," Savage pointed out. "In fact, the idea that she did have her was pretty wild in the first place. What would be her motive? Even if she did want to scare you into backing off from your investigation, kidnapping your friend would be an awfully bold move."

"I know. I guess we're chasing windmills with this one. Still, I think I'm going to ask her if she's seen Victoria."

"Don't you think that will seem suspicious? Remember, we don't want her to know we consider her to be a suspect in this whole thing."

"So you don't think she's guilty?"

"No, I don't. Brooke is a very sweet, hardworking person. I'm not saying your theory doesn't have merit; I just can't see Brooke being the monster she'd have to be to kill three people—four if you count Katrina—and kidnap Victoria. She might turn out to be a viable suspect, but I think we should keep looking."

"I guess you're right."

Savage started my car just as my phone beeped, letting me know I had a text. "It's Brit. She says Victoria is home."

Savage turned the car around and drove back to the sheriff's station. He got out and I climbed into the driver's seat to head for home.

Chapter 14

I found Victoria packing her suitcase. "Are you going somewhere?"

"Hawaii," Victoria answered. She had just gotten out of the shower and looked like a teenager, with her wet hair that tended to curl on its own, cutoff jeans, and bright yellow sweatshirt. "Brad called, suggesting we take an earlier flight. It seemed like a good idea, so I agreed."

I looked at Vikki's face, which was presently devoid of even a trace of makeup. I could always tell when she was lying, and it looked like she'd been crying. I sat down on the edge of the bed. "What's really going on?"

"Nothing. Like I said, Brad and I have decided to leave for our trip earlier than planned. We really do have a lot to discuss before we meet with his backers. Getting a movie deal is a huge undertaking and I don't want to take it lightly."

"I've been calling and texting you for hours."

Vikki averted her eyes. "I guess I must have forgotten to turn on my phone. I turned it off during dinner last night."

"If you turned off your phone how did Brad manage to call you about the change in plans?"

Vikki stopped what she was doing and turned to look at me. I could see she knew I knew she was lying.

"Did something happen last night?"

Vikki set the blouse she was folding on the bed and sat down next to me. "I guess you know I stayed at Rick's last night."

"He mentioned it. Was it bad?"

"It was worse than bad, it was really, really amazing."

"And that scared you?"

Vikki took my hand in hers. "Of course it scared me. You know how commitment-phobic I am. The guy is a babe and I figured the sex would be nice, but I wasn't expecting amazing. And that wasn't even the worst part."

"The amazing sex wasn't the worst part?"

"It was the before and the after. He was so attentive and polite and so incredibly sweet. Most guys roll over and go to sleep when the main event has reached its natural conclusion, but Rick held me in his arms and caressed my hair until I fell asleep. Or at least until I faked going to sleep. I'm certain I've never been treated quite so tenderly in my life. I'm not going to see him again."

"He had no way to know how skittish you are, and it was only one date."

"Yes, but it was an amazing date."

"Having an amazing date doesn't mean you have to stop seeing the guy. I'm sure if you explain to him that you're only in to really crappy dates, he can make adjustments."

Victoria smiled. "I guess I am being kind of ridiculous."

"Very ridiculous. He sounds wonderful, even if he does occasionally get on my nerves."

Victoria laid back in the bed and pulled the pillow to her chest, giving it a hug. "It really was a magical evening. Not only was the attraction between us extremely intense but we had so much in common. We talked and talked over dinner and never once experienced an awkward silence. Rick is smart and funny and so attentive. He really is the perfect guy. And for a while I was so very content. But then, after Rick fell asleep, I started to have all these thoughts about the future, and I realized that even though I'd only known him a few hours I already really wanted him to be part of my future. I'm not used to caring about the men I sleep with, and I guess I had a bit of a meltdown. I snuck downstairs and called a cab. I didn't want him to come down and find me waiting for the cab because that would have been just too humiliating, so I had the cab company pick me up down the street. While I was waiting for the cab I turned on my phone, and there was a message from Brad saying he was on the island and wanted to talk. I called him and he was close by, so I had him come get me."

"So you spent the rest of the night with Brad?"

Vikki pulled the pillow over her face. She let out a long groan. "Yes, I guess I did. I really am a horrible person."

"You aren't a horrible person."

Vikki pulled the pillow down. "Maybe not, but when I woke up this morning I knew I needed some distance from Rick to sort through my feelings, so I asked Brad if it would work for us to move our trip up and he was open to the idea. I told him to book us a flight tonight and I came home to pack."

"And you were going to leave without telling anyone?"

"I was going to leave a note."

"I think you might owe Rick Savage more than a note. He was really worried about you. We both were."

Vikki hung her head. "I'm sorry, Jilli. I wasn't thinking. I never meant to worry you. I just needed some time to deal with the deep emotions Rick awakened. I was, and am, completely overwhelmed."

Wow. It seemed like love-'em-and-leave-'em Victoria Vance really had fallen for the guy. "I know you're feeling out of your depth, but you should talk to him, tell him you're leaving."

"I'm too embarrassed to face him. Will you explain it to him in a way that won't make him hate me?"

"It'll mean more coming from you."

"I can't."

"Okay. I guess I can talk to him. That is, after all, what best friends are for. But if I were you, instead of running away from your emotions, you might take a minute to ask yourself why the emotions exist in the first place. Maybe, after all this time, you've finally found the guy you've been looking for."

******

After Vikki left I called Savage to filled him in. I told him he was still welcome to come to the meeting that evening, but he declined. I could tell by the tone in his voice that the poor man was hurt. Not that I blamed him. Vikki was a fantastic friend, but she'd always been a pretty terrible girlfriend to the men who migrated in and out of her life. I remembered we'd never gone over the coroner's report, but I figured it could wait one more day, especially now that the gang was beginning to gather.

That evening's meeting was centered on the *how*. If one of the kids had killed Rayleen, Trevor, and Joshua, how had they done it? And, more importantly, how had they convinced the others to give such different stories to the cops? The idea that the survivors had intentionally given different accountings to confuse the sheriff's department was really the only thing that made sense.

"What if they were all in on it?" Alex suggested. "That would explain why they banded together to mislead the deputy who interviewed them."

"So you think there was a plot or conspiracy to kill these three kids?" I asked.

"No, not necessarily. Maybe Troy killed Rayleen in a fit of rage after he caught her flirting with Trevor. And then maybe Trevor went after Troy and during the course of the altercation, Trevor fell into the anchor and impaled himself, or maybe someone pushed him. Maybe the survivors made a pact not to tell, but Joshua, who wasn't one of them, threatened to tell, so he was killed as well."

"That actually makes sense," I admitted. "Impossible to prove unless we can get someone to confess, though."

"So who's the weakest link?" Alex asked.

"Carrie. She seemed pretty timid when I spoke to her earlier in the week. I guess I can try talking to her again."

"Let me try," Alex offered. "I have a way with women."

I rolled my eyes. Alex was as cocky as he was rich and good-looking.

"Even if they were all in on the cover-up eleven years ago it still doesn't explain who killed Katrina," Brit pointed out.

"Brit has a point," I acknowledged. "If we go with Alex's theory are we to assume that Troy, Jason, Brooklyn, and Carrie are all responsible for killing Katrina and sending me threatening notes?"

No one answered, I imagined because no one had an answer.

"We don't actually know that Katrina's death is related to the deaths eleven years ago," Charles said.

"It would be pretty amazing if it weren't," I countered. "If Katrina had died on some random date at some random time, maybe."

What I really wanted to do was share my theory about Brooklyn, but I'd promised Savage I wouldn't. Though if the group came to the conclusion on their own that Brooklyn was the killer, I probably wouldn't be breaking my promise by agreeing with them. "If we assume there's just one killer and we assume it's one of the five survivors, who would it most likely be?"

"Troy," Alex said right away.

"I agree," Brit joined in. "Rayleen was Troy's girlfriend and he was angry with her for flirting with Trevor. He had the most motive of any of the survivors to want them dead."

"And Joshua?" I asked.

"Maybe he stumbled onto Troy while he was killing the others," Charles said, jumping on the Troy bandwagon."

"And you did receive your first warning note shortly after visiting him at the bank," Clara added.

Everyone was making good points. Maybe it *had* been Troy and not Brooke. Somehow I found myself really hoping that was true.

******

Jack had been late to the meeting, but he lingered after everyone retired to their private quarters. I was feeling emotionally drained and figured I could use someone to talk to, so I opened a bottle of wine and we settled on the deck. It was a beautiful night, warm and clear. The moon shone down on the calm sea as small waves lapped gently onto the shore. Clara had said another storm was coming, but from where I sat the night was about as perfect as perfect could be.

"I have something I wanted to talk to you about but waited until we were alone because I promised Savage you would be the only one I would speak to about this specific subject."

"Okay; shoot."

"First of all, I found out that a man named Jimmy Breelin was friends with Katrina when they were kids. He told me the reason Katrina even started hanging out with Carrie was to get close to Brooklyn. According to Jimmy, Katrina was in love with her."

"Do you think Brooklyn knew how Katrina felt?"

"Jimmy said no. He said Katrina was a very private person who mostly hung back in the shadows. He didn't think she would actually have approached Brooklyn with her feelings, but she might have been watching from afar. That made me think about the poem. What if Brooklyn did kill Rayleen, Trevor, and Joshua, and what if Katrina saw her do it?"

"And you think Katrina confronted her after all this time?"

"I don't know. Maybe. I know that doesn't really make sense, but I spoke to Blackbeard this morning and was able to determine that when he said 'pickles and cream' he meant he saw a pregnant woman. Brooklyn, who's now Brooke

Johnson, is pregnant. What if Katrina did see her kill those kids and for whatever reason decided to confront her with what she knew after all these years? Maybe she freaked out and pushed her off the pier, killing her when she hit the rocks below?"

Jack didn't respond right away. It was a lot to take in. I would be having an easier time with this theory if we hadn't met Brooke. She really was the sweetest thing. And she wasn't just nice but a good mom who gave back to her community. Even though I really thought it was her, I didn't want it to be.

Jack finally replied. "What you say makes sense, but part of the reason you went down this road in the first place was because of the poem you found. Katrina wrote thousands of poems, many of which she posted online. It seems a stretch to randomly choose one poem out of the whole bunch and decide that it's related to the Massacre. It could very well have been about something totally unrelated. In fact, when you take the timeline into it, it most likely had nothing whatsoever to do with Katrina's death."

"I guess you might be right," I admitted.

"You've given me an idea, though. Katrina not only wrote thousands of poems, she took thousands of photos. Some are posted online or hanging in her gallery, but I bet she has tons of others stored in boxes or on data-storage units. Maybe it would be worth our while to go to Charleston to talk to her sister. She seemed open and receptive to talking when I called her. She might be able to give us some insight into what was going on with Katrina during her final days. She might also let us look around a bit. I bet the photos and poetry *not* posted will reveal more than the things she did post."

"That seems like a good plan," I agreed. "When do you want to go?"

"Tomorrow? We can make a day of it. Maybe have lunch and walk around the Historic District."

"This isn't another lame attempt at a date, is it?"

Jack grinned. "Now, would I do that after you so clearly told me that you weren't under any circumstances interested?"

"Knowing you, turning a day of investigation into a date is exactly what you would do."

Chapter 15

Wednesday, October 18

Jack planned to pick me up at the house later that morning, but I figured I had enough time to run by Savage's office to see what information, if any, we could find from the autopsy reports filed for Rayleen, Trevor, and Joshua. I knew there hadn't been anything significant enough to point to a specific killer or that person would have been arrested years ago, but it couldn't hurt to set a new pair of eyes on the situation. I just hoped Savage wasn't too broken up about the way Victoria had treated him.

"Good morning," I said as I set the bag of doughnuts I'd brought as a peace offering on Savage's desk.

"I thought I might see you. Thanks for the doughnuts." Savage opened the bag and took out a maple bar.

"You're very welcome. Jack and I are going into Charleston for the day, but I wanted to see if you'd found anything noteworthy on the autopsy reports."

Savage passed me a folder. I opened it and grimaced when I realized there were photos attached to the reports. Ignoring them, I scanned down to the summary. Rayleen had been stabbed in the back thirteen times. It appeared her assailant had stood over her; the angle of the knife was determined to have been delivered in a downward thrust.

"It almost seems like she was kneeling on the ground," I commented. "Do you think this was carried out gangland style?" The thought of making a teenager kneel on the ground before stabbing her to death made my stomach churn. I found myself regretting the second doughnut I'd eaten on the drive over.

"It looks like that might have been the case. I suppose she may have been kneeling for some other reason, but without an eyewitness we may never know."

"It also said she had bruising on various parts of her body. As if she'd been in a fight."

"I went back to recheck the report filed by the original deputy. Brooklyn Vanderbilt also showed signs of having been in a fight. She told the investigator she'd fought with Rayleen earlier in the day, before they even arrived on Waverly

Island. The other survivors confirmed that was true."

I hated that everything seemed to be coming back around to Brooke. I couldn't imagine what it would be like to have your baby taken away from you while you rotted away in prison for something that had happened so long ago.

The autopsy report for Trevor Bailey confirmed that he'd fallen or been pushed onto the anchor. There weren't any additional wounds to indicate that he'd been in a fight prior to being impaled. Given the fact that he'd fallen backward, it really did seem he'd been pushed. In most cases when someone simply tripped they fell forward.

The report also confirmed that both Trevor and Joshua had a significant amount of alcohol in their systems when they died. Both boys had also smoked marijuana within an hour of their deaths. The autopsy report on Joshua indicated he'd drowned. He was found facedown in a pool of water; given his state of intoxication, he could very well have simply passed out, falling face-first into the pond.

I pushed the file back across the desk. "I guess there isn't much here. Knowing that Rayleen was stabbed from behind and was most likely on her knees when she was killed is disturbing. Based on what I've learned about her, I was imagining she was stabbed during an altercation. I even thought she might have been stabbed in self-defense, but that doesn't appear to be the case."

"The more we dig into this, the more I wonder if we even should," Savaged commented.

"You're thinking Brooke really is the killer."

"The investigation does keep coming back to her. I didn't know her back when the Massacre happened, but I know her now. I know how it looks, but I just can't reconcile the fact that this woman could have killed her peers in cold blood."

"Jack and I are going to talk to Katrina's sister today. Maybe she'll have some insight that will put a new twist on things. Are you going to talk to Brooke?"

"I think I might ask her about the fight she had with Rayleen. Like you, I felt slightly better about things when I was able to tell myself Rayleen's death was a result of her assailant defending herself, but now that I know she was stabbed from behind..." Savage shook his head.

I knew exactly how he felt. As badly as I wanted to solve this mystery and report it to the world, there was a part of me that really didn't want to know what had happened on the tragic day eleven years before.

******

Charleston is a beautiful town steeped in culture and history. I'd visited a few times before I moved to Gull Island and had always enjoyed spending time in the Historic District. The brick buildings and horse-drawn carriages created the illusion that you'd stepped back in time. The gallery Katrina had opened was just a block from the aquarium, so we parked in the garage and walked down the crowded street. I'd called ahead to make sure it would be open given Katrina's recent death and been told her sister was planning to operate it as a tribute to Katrina for the foreseeable future.

As with the work she'd posted online, the pieces displayed in Katrina's gallery were dark and edgy. Each seemed to have just enough emotional rawness to catch your eye, while the depth of understanding portrayed continued to hold your interest. Looking at Katrina's art was like looking in to her soul, where her emotion was boldly displayed for all to see. Most of her work was in black and white, which somehow gave it a primal feel that color prints never would.

"This stuff is really good," Jack commented. "Disturbing but good."

"I know. Looking at her work both horrifies and mesmerizes me. I want to look away, but I can't. She really had a way of capturing the human condition in its basest form."

"I wonder if Katrina's sister is here."

I looked around but didn't see anyone who looked like the photo I'd seen of Katrina. "I guess it can't hurt to ask the man speaking to the couple in the front if she's available. What's her name?"

"Shelley Moore."

"Excuse me," I said to the man who was showing several prints to an older couple. "Is Shelley Moore in today?"

"Are you friends of hers?"

"No. But we spoke to her on the phone and told her we wanted to speak to her about Katrina's work, and she seemed to be willing to chat with us."

"She's working over in the framing shop. It's not far. A couple blocks over. You best call first because she'll probably be in the back. If she knows you're coming she can unlock the door." The man handed me a business card. "Here's her number."

"Thank you. You've been very helpful."

As he'd suggested, we walked to the shop. It was a beautiful day and it felt good to be out and about, enjoying the sunshine. That was one thing my old life in New York hadn't afforded me: time to simply go outside and take a long, leisurely walk.

"It's too bad we don't have more time. Some of these shops look interesting," I commented.

"Do you like to window-shop?"

"Actually, no. When I worked at the newspaper I was busy all the time, so I never had time for regular shopping. Let alone window-shopping. But now that my daily schedule has opened up somewhat, I realize that looking through the eclectic shops in the Historic District might make for an interesting afternoon."

"Do you miss it? The hustle and bustle of your old life?"

"Actually, I do. In fact, it's occurred to me on more than one occasion that I should have stayed in New York and tried to get another job right away, rather than running away to Gull Island. Not that I don't enjoy my life on the island, but the change of pace has been a big adjustment. Still, I do look forward to going back, and I do have this fantasy that my old boss will realize what a horrible mistake he made letting me go and beg me to come back."

"And would you? Go back if offered a job?"

I stepped to the side to allow two young boys on bikes to pass. "I guess it depends on the timing. I know I would definitely consider it, although I do feel I've made a commitment to Garrett to stay until the remodel is completed and he can put a manager in place. If an offer ever actually came through I'd have to consider all my options. I enjoy being part of the writers' group. Before moving to Gull Island, I never had time for friends other than Victoria. Do you miss living in the city?"

"Not at all. The slower pace on Gull Island suits me perfectly. It's hard to know what life will bring, but at this point I feel I've found a place to settle in and call home."

Jack opened the door and motioned for me to enter ahead of him. The shop had large windows that let in the sunshine that reflected off long tables with frames in various stages of assembly. The sound of a saw in the background paired nicely with the smell of lacquer and wood dust that greeted us.

"Hello," Jack called, not wanting, I was certain, to try to let ourselves into the back without permission.

The sound of the saw stilled. "Is someone there?"

"It's Jackson Jones and Jillian Hanford."

"Come on back. I'm elbow deep in sawdust."

I followed Jack down a short hallway that opened up into a large room with a variety of saws as well as several long tables that looked to be used for staining and assembling.

"I'm sorry I'm such a mess." Shelley attempted to wipe the sawdust from her cheek with her forearm, but she only smeared it, making it worse. "I've been working around the clock, trying to get everything ready for the show."

"Show?" I asked.

"Katrina had been asked to participate in a big art show in New York next month. It was her dream." The smile faded from Shelley's face. "I can't believe she's going to miss it."

"I'm very sorry for your loss," I said. In my mind the fact that Katrina had a show coming up that she'd very much wanted to attend negated the idea that she'd committed suicide.

"We won't keep you long." Jack smiled at her, which helped return the smile to her own face. "We were in town and happened to stop by the gallery. Being in the midst of Katrina's work brought up some additional questions."

"I could use a break. There's a small room in the back. I have sodas if you're thirsty."

"Thank you; that would be nice," Jack answered as we followed Shelley down another little hallway.

After she brought us our beverages and we all sat down at the table she asked what we wanted to know. I could see she was trying to put on a positive front, but she looked tired and her eyes were swollen. I wasn't sure I'd want to be working if my sister had just died, but perhaps getting Katrina's work ready for the show was a way of grieving and offering a tribute at the same time.

"As I mentioned to you when we spoke on the phone, Jillian and I are working on a story, or more accurately a couple of stories, about Katrina. We want to focus on her life rather than just her death, so we'd like to find out as much as we can about her. Not only who she was as a teen but who she became," Jack began. "When we visited the gallery today and were able to experience firsthand the depth of emotion her work expressed, it occurred to us that the woman we'd been planning to write about had a lot more layers than we first imagined."

"Katrina definitely felt things deeply. Too deeply. She took on the pain of the world and made it her own. She had her art as an outlet for the suffering she seemed so willing to open herself up to, but to be honest, I never thought it was enough."

"What do you mean, it wasn't enough?" I asked.

"Katrina lived a difficult life filled with the images she captured on film but could never quite get out of her mind. People aren't meant to take on the suffering of others the way she did. It was too much for one person to bear."

"The Massacre must have been exceptionally difficult for her," I said.

"It was a very hard time. Katrina withdrew from the world. I know she worked on her poetry, but she never published any of it. I think it was too painful even for her."

"She seemed to be doing well now," I pointed out.

"She was. It seemed she'd found a way to compartmentalize the pain and suffering she witnessed every day, but then the nightmares started up again. I tried to get her to see a therapist, but she refused. I could see I was losing her to the demons in her head, and after I found her passed out on her sofa after taking too many sleeping pills, I hired an attorney and filed a petition that would require her to seek professional help. My request was granted and Katrina started seeing a wonderful woman who used regression techniques to help her deal with the demons in her past. At first it seemed to be working. Katrina was eating and sleeping better. She started working on her art again and used her savings to open the gallery. I really thought she'd turned a corner, and then the next thing I knew, I received a call saying she'd been found dead at the foot of a pier on Gull Island."

"And you have no idea why she went back to the island?" I asked.

"No. She never even mentioned she was going to be away from the gallery that day. I'm not sure if the trip was planned or she spontaneously decided to go."

"What about any events immediately preceding the trip?" Jack asked.

"I know she went to see her therapist that morning." Shelley settled back in her chair before she continued. "Normally, Katrina went to counseling on Tuesdays, but the therapist wanted her to come in an extra time that week because the anniversary of the Friday the Thirteenth Massacre was coming up. It wasn't just an annual anniversary, you know. This year was the first time the thirteenth fell on a Friday in October since the Massacre."

"Yes, I realized that," I answered. "Do you know what Katrina and her therapist talked about?"

"No. She wouldn't say. She did seem to be upset that Katrina had gone to the island, but I guess that's normal considering the way things turned out."

"Did Katrina keep a diary?" I asked. "Perhaps she wrote about her plans."

"She might have kept one in addition to her poetry. I'm really not sure. I know she posted a lot of stuff on her website. Poetry and such. To be honest, this whole thing has been a bit too real for me to deal with. I'm not sure I'm ready to read Katrina's thoughts on the eve of her death. I guess I should at some point. I'm not sure what was going through her mind that would convince her it would be a good idea to return to Gull Island on that particular day, but I guess if I want to understand I'll eventually need to find out if she left any clues."

I looked around the room. I could see this conversation was very difficult for Shelley. In a way, I was sorry Jack and I had come to see her in the first place. Yes, we both had stories to write, but it didn't feel right that we should have them at someone else's expense. Maybe I was getting soft in my old age.

"The photos in the gallery: Are they all Katrina had, or did she keep some back?" Jack asked.

"The photos in the gallery are just the tip of the iceberg. Katrina took thousands and thousands of photos. Most are stored in those boxes lined up on the wall. Of course the more recent photos are all digitized."

"Are the photos organized in any way?" I asked. "Either by subject or date?"

"There are dates on the boxes as well as the digital files Was there anything you were particularly interested in?"

"The photos from the time just prior to and including the death of those kids eleven years ago might be a good place to start. It really does seem that whatever happened last Friday could be linked to the events of that day. Katrina had a way of capturing random moments. She might have caught something on film that could provide a clue to what happened."

"Help yourself." Shelley gestured toward the stacks of boxes. "I imagine if Katrina had any photos she didn't want seen she wouldn't have brought them down here."

Jack and I spent the next thirty minutes looking through the box we estimated would contain the photos we were looking for. It appeared Katrina took photos of anything and everything. Some of the photos were exceptional, while others were unremarkable. There were photos taken at school in Town, and at home. I did notice there were a lot of photos of Brooklyn. I doubted she even knew she was being photographed. They didn't appear to be posed and Brooklyn wasn't looking directly at the camera. The idea that Katrina followed her around, snapping photos of the moments of her life, seemed to be more real now that we'd seen the physical proof. I wondered if Brooklyn had had any idea she had a stalker, and if she did know I wondered if it bothered her.

Due to the sheer volume of photos I wasn't sure we'd be able to distinguish the relevant from the irrelevant, but I noticed a stack of photos that appeared to have been taken earlier on the day the kids went sailing. Many were fun photos of the kids drinking and frolicking around, as teens were apt to do. It looked like they were having a good time before the storm hit and ruined their plans. There was a photo of Jason talking to Trevor that had been taken on the pier. Based on the clothing they were wearing, it had been taken on the same day, although I didn't see anyone else around; perhaps the guys had shown up early. There was another one of just Jason doing something at the control panel.

"Look at this." I handed the photo to Jack.

"Carrie told me the radio didn't work that day, but Deputy Savage said the radio had been working the previous day, that someone had pulled out the wires. Doesn't this look like Jason pulling wires out of the control panel?"

Jack frowned and took a second look at the photo. "That could be the radio, but why would Jason disable the radio on his dad's boat?"

"It's bothered me that Jason, who was an experienced sailor who'd lived on the island his entire life, hadn't paid more attention to the weather report and started back sooner. What if it was his intention to end up stranded on Waverly Island in the first place?"

"Why would he want to do that?"

"I don't know," I admitted. "But the fact that they were intentionally stranded makes more sense than that a boat full of kids who knew the water and the area would end up being stranded by a storm that had been predicted."

"I guess we can make a copy of the photo and ask Jason about it," Jack suggested.

"He's up north visiting his mama and I don't know when he'll be back."

"He isn't up north. He got a job at Conway Marine. I called him to verify a few facts and he told me he started there a week ago."

"Troy called Conway Marine seconds after I left his office when I interviewed him on Monday. He must have been calling Jason."

"Well, if you were asking about the day those kids died and Jason and his buddies did intentionally strand them on the island, he could have been giving him a heads-up. That's worth looking in to."

"Yeah," I agreed. "That sounds like a good idea indeed."

Jack asked Shelley if she had a copier on the premises, and whether she would mind if we made copies of a couple of the photos we'd found. She did and didn't mind, sending me to a copier in a little room at the back of the building that Katrina had used as a business office. I headed there while Jack remained behind to put the boxes back where we'd found them.

The copier was on the corner of the desk, next to the phone. I placed the photo in the copier, then noticed a handwritten note near the phone: Brooke's name and a phone number. Under that someone, probably Katrina, had also written *Thompson's Pier*. It looked like I had just found what I needed to prove Brooke had been the pregnant woman who'd met with Katrina the day she died.

Chapter 16

Jack and I stopped by Conway Marine on the way back to Gull Island only to be told that something had come up and Jason had had to leave early. Jack had found another photo of interest while he'd been putting everything away. In addition to the one showing Jason tampering with the radio, he'd discovered one that must have been taken the next day, showing Jason putting something wrapped in a sweatshirt into the boat's cargo hold. Could it have been the murder weapon? The really odd thing was that Katrina appeared in the background of the second photo, which meant someone else had used Katrina's camera to take it.

I called Savage to tell him what we'd discovered. He asked us to drop off the photos at his office on the way home. Savage verified what I suspected: Jason no longer owned the boat he'd borrowed from his father, and unless someone came forward to tell us what had been wrapped in the sweatshirt, there was no way of finding out at this point. He did say it appeared Jason had intentionally tampered with the radio and assured us he would follow up with him as soon as he could track him down.

Jack had just dropped me off at home when I received a text from Brooke: She was ready to share the whole story of the Massacre and wanted me to meet her, alone. I knew she could very well be luring me into a trap, but the reporter inside got the better of me and I headed out to my car and drove in the direction Brooke had indicated.

When I got to the building, which was located at the end of a deserted road, I saw several cars in the drive. I was on the verge of turning around and heading back home when Brooke walked up to the open front door and motioned me to come inside.

I had a decision to make. The fact that Brooke seemed to be willing to hand me the information I hadn't been able to get on my own seemed suspect. Maybe this was a trap; maybe she was setting me up to take a fall. It certainly wouldn't be the first time someone had handed me information just when I needed it only to have it backfire on me. But if I was ever going to get my life in New York back I needed this story, and despite my best efforts, I hadn't been able to find the proof I needed to bring the story home. I could hear Brooke out and then decide what to do with the information. Deep down inside, I really didn't think she planned to kill me, so I grabbed my tape recorder and headed to the door.

When I entered I saw Troy, Carrie, and a man I assumed from the photos I'd seen was Jason, waiting for me. I glanced at Brooke, who motioned for me to have a seat at the table they had gathered around.

"We brought you here to tell you the story, the true story of what occurred on Waverly Island when Rayleen, Trevor, and Joshua died," Brooke began. "The secret has been kept too long already; for any of us to find peace it must be told. We talked about it and decided to share it with you. Once you know what happened, it will be up to you to decide what to do with it, but we all hope you'll treat the information we're about to reveal with the sensitivity it deserves."

"Okay." I glanced around the table. Carrie appeared to be terrified, Troy reluctant, Jason guarded, and Brooke resigned.

"That day, Jason and Trevor hatched a plan to get Carrie and me alone on a deserted island for a night of sexual fun. Not only did they pack a whole lot of booze but they brought along drugs meant to loosen our inhibitions. Jason knew a storm was coming, so he came up with the idea to strand us on Waverly Island for the night. The original plan was for only the two couples to go off on this excursion."

I glanced at Jason, whose lips were pursed with tension. He wouldn't make eye contact with me, didn't react to what Brooke had said in any way. I didn't think telling me this story was his idea.

"The problem with the guys' plan was that my cousin Joshua was visiting and my father had asked me to keep him occupied," Brooke continued. "When I told Trevor Joshua would have to come with us he told Carrie the trip might have to be postponed. She decided to invite Katrina to even things out."

Brooke took a deep breath before going on. The others simply sat and waited, but I could see everyone was tense. I couldn't blame them.

"Rayleen had learned about the sailing trip from Trevor, who'd mentioned it to her in passing. Although Trevor and I were dating, I think he always had a thing for Rayleen, who was much more sexually uninhibited than I ever was going to be. I almost didn't go along when Rayleen showed up at the marina with Troy because I hated her more than I'd ever hated anyone on earth. But I didn't want to leave Trevor alone with that witch, so I went along to protect what was mine."

"Why did you hate her so much?" I asked.

"A teacher who meant everything to me was fired because of her lies."

I remembered that a teacher had been fired after Rayleen had accused him of sexual assault. "The teacher who was fired—were you having an affair with him?"

"No. Scott would never do that. He was just there for me when no one else was. My mother wasn't around a whole lot when I was growing up and my dad was either working or at the bar. I didn't have anyone I could talk to. And then I met this kind, amazing teacher who actually seemed to care whether I passed or failed. He tutored me and encouraged me. He took an interest in me and changed my life. I was such a mess before he came to the island, but he convinced me I was smart and had a lot to offer. He made me want to succeed. And then Rayleen came along and told a bunch of lies just because she was flunking his class and he wouldn't change her grade. I was devastated when he was forced to leave the island. I went a little off the deep end, so my dad sent me to stay with my mother. I ended up being with her for a year and had just returned to Gull Island a couple of months before the sailing trip."

Brooke paused. I could see her poised persona was beginning to crumble. "Back to the story. If I don't get this out now I never will."

"I'm sorry. Please continue."

"After Jason, who we later found out had tampered with the radio, announced that we were going to have to wait out the storm on a deserted island, the mood began to change from unrestrained pleasure to fear and uncertainty."

"To be fair," Jason spoke up for the first time, "while I suppose Trevor and I could be faulted for coming up with such an elaborate plan to get into our girlfriends' pants, neither of us realized how strong the storm would be. We were looking for a night of erotic pleasure, not death and horror."

Brooke gave Jason a dirty look. "Yes, well, I guess when you hatch a plan that includes drugging your girlfriend you should expect any unpleasantness that comes your way." She looked back in my direction. "Anyway, after we landed on the island we found a structure we felt would provide the most protection. There was a lot of scrap wood lying around and a couple of the guys had matches, so we started a fire. After we settled in a bit some of the tension left us and we were actually having a pretty good time."

Brooke glanced at Troy. "Then Rayleen started flirting with Trevor and he was flirting right back. I didn't say anything at the time, although I was furious, but Troy wasn't having anything to do with Trevor feeling up his girl, so he made several very pointed comments. That made Rayleen mad and she started badgering Troy, which angered Jason, who was getting somewhere with Carrie, so he told them to knock it off. Rayleen headed out into the storm. I was angry and wanted to make it very clear to her that it wasn't okay for her to have her hands all over my boyfriend, so I followed her. We argued and then she slapped me. I slapped her back. I already hated Rayleen so much that I went sort of crazy. The next thing I knew, we were punching each other and wrestling around in the mud."

A single tear slid down Brooke's face. She glanced at each person at the table before speaking again. It almost looked as if she was verifying that they still wanted her to continue. I saw Carrie nod, which seemed to give Brooke new resolve.

"Rayleen was a bully who fought all the time and was a lot better at it than I was. It didn't take long for her to have me pinned to the ground, and she started to choke me. I really thought she was going to choke me to death. I was almost to the point of passing out when suddenly she screamed and let go of my neck. I rolled away and saw Katrina with a knife. She was stabbing Rayleen over and over again."

I gasped, while tears streamed down Brooke's face.

"I was in shock and just sat there in the mud and pouring rain and watched Katrina stab the life from Rayleen. Eventually, she must have realized what she was doing because she dropped the knife and ran off into the storm. The next few minutes seemed like a dream. I picked up the knife and walked over to Rayleen's body. I knelt down to check for a pulse. I was so scared and didn't know what to do, so I dragged her over to a tree and leaned her up against it. I just stood there sobbing, and the lightning was getting closer and I knew I had to go back. I turned around to head back to the building when I saw Trevor was watching me. I guess he'd come out after me at some point. I don't know how much he saw, but he definitely saw me standing over the body. He kept saying, 'What did you do, what did you do?' over and over again. I kept screaming that I didn't do anything, but he wouldn't listen. He just kept yelling at me. I was totally flipping out by that point. He grabbed my arm and I pushed him. He'd been drinking and wasn't all that steady on his feet, so he stumbled backward a few steps, then tripped on something and fell back onto the anchor."

Brooke was sobbing hysterically. "I didn't mean to kill him. I just wanted to make him stop yelling at me."

Oh God.

"I was so scared that I just ran. Then I found Katrina, who was sitting in the rain just staring into space. I tried to talk to her, to tell her that it wasn't her fault, that she'd saved my life, but she was so traumatized I wasn't sure she understood what I was saying. Eventually, I managed to get her back to the building where the others were waiting. I told them what had happened and they were almost as freaked out as Katrina and me."

"Where had Katrina gotten the knife?" I asked.

"It was there on the ground. The place where Rayleen and I were fighting must have been some sort of a dump. Not only was the knife on the ground and the old anchor nearby but there were all sorts of other old, rusted objects."

"What about Joshua? Was he with the others when you returned with Katrina?" I asked.

"No. He wasn't there. We found his body later. Unless someone knows something I don't, it really does seem that he just got drunk and headed into the storm, where he passed out from all the booze he'd drunk and drowned."

I glanced at each person at the table. None of them seemed to be exhibiting body language that would indicated the story Brooke was telling wasn't the truth. "Go on," I encouraged. "What happened next?"

"We all sat around wondering what to do, wondering what would happen. Would Katrina go to jail for killing Rayleen, even though she'd saved my life? Would I go to jail for killing Trevor, even though I'd just pushed him away and he'd lost his footing and fallen onto the anchor? Would the police believe Joshua had simply drowned? Would Jason be in trouble for disabling the radio to trick Carrie and me? Troy and Carrie hadn't really done anything wrong, but we were all scared."

Brooke paused and took a sip of water. She was through the worst of it, but I sensed she had more to say.

"The night seemed to go on and on and on, and we talked about all the things that might happen, and we freaked ourselves out even more than we already were. Katrina was the worst. She was totally flipping out, so I tried something I honestly wasn't sure would work. I took her face in my hands and told her I could help her. I told her she had to trust me. She nodded, so I hugged her and told her everything was going to be okay, and then I hypnotized her and gave her a new memory based part on fact and part on fiction. In her new memory she hadn't killed Rayleen."

"Hypnotized her?" I asked. "But you were just a kid. How did you know how to do that?"

"My mother is Gabriella Vanhousen."

"Gabriella Vanhousen, the hypnotist?"

"Yes. She has her own show in Las Vegas. When my dad sent me to stay with her and we got to know each other better, she told me that I had the gift. Not everyone can do what she does, you know. She taught me how to put people under and then offer them a suggestion. I wasn't sure it would work with Katrina, but it did. She was in such a vulnerable state, I think she was more than receptive to the suggestion that an unknown killer and not her had killed Rayleen."

"Okay, but what about everyone else? The witness statements you gave were all so different."

"We decided to each come up with a similar but different story. We figured if we all told something somewhat different, the sheriff wouldn't be able to sort out fact from fiction. And it worked. After they talked to each of us the investigation was all but dropped; we all seemed to have such different memories, there was no physical evidence, and there was no proof there was anyone else on the island."

I looked at Carrie. "When I spoke to you the other day you didn't seem to be lying about what you remembered."

"I wasn't. Brooke relaxed us into a state where we were open to suggestion and then she helped us build new memories. Later, after we returned to Gull Island, I really was confused about what I remembered and what I'd made up."

"Brooke's hocus pocus didn't work as well on me," Jason admitted, "but I was fine with lying."

Wow. The story I was being told was a lot more complicated than I expected the truth could be.

"Who's been sending me the threatening notes?" I asked.

"That would be me," Troy admitted. "When you came to see me at the bank I suddenly remembered everything. It was like a light went on. I remembered exactly what happened, including our plan to cover things up."

"So you called Jason."

"Yeah. How'd you know?"

"I traced the call."

Troy frowned.

"I'm a reporter," I reminded him. "So what about Katrina? What happened on the pier?"

I glanced at Brooke, who had new tears streaming down her face. Oh God, she *had* killed her. I really didn't want Brooke to be the bad guy.

"Katrina called me last Friday," Brooke began in a quiet little voice. "She wanted me to meet her on the pier. She said her memories—her real memories—were coming back and it wouldn't be long before her court-appointed therapist found out what was locked inside her head. The poor thing was so scared. I guess she'd been having nightmares about that night and she was beginning to remember what really happened." Brooke wiped the tears from her face with the back of her hand, then looked directly at me. "Katrina was in love with me when we were in high school. She never said as much and I pretended not to know, but I did. She used to follow me around, lurking in the shadows, watching me, even taking photos of me. On the night Rayleen and I fought, Katrina had followed me into the storm, which was how she was there to help me in the first place. I thought I was helping her by erasing her memory of what had occurred, but I guess in the long run I did just the opposite. Katrina was a deeply emotional, deeply disturbed person even before what happened on Waverly Island. I masked her memory, but I guess her subconscious knew what really happened and it tortured her. I learned she'd had already tried to commit suicide once, which was why she was seeing the therapist in the first place." Brooke looked me in the eye. "I wasn't trying to hurt her; I was trying to help her, but in the end I killed her."

"You killed her?"

"Not literally. But I'm responsible for her death. If I hadn't messed around with her mind she'd still be alive."

"What happened?" I asked.

"When I arrived at the pier Katrina told me that she remembered what had really happened. She told me that she was grateful I'd tried to help her, but she couldn't live with the fact that she'd taken a life. She looked me in the eye, kissed me on the lips, told me that she loved me, and jumped."

Chapter 17

By the time I got home I felt numb. I was faced with a horrible dilemma. On one hand, I had a story that would open the doors I needed to get back my old life, which was something I'd thought I very much wanted. The problem was that if I published the story, Brooke could be charged with manslaughter in Trevor's death. In addition, she could face charges for intentionally interfering with a murder investigation. There was the real possibility she could go to jail and her baby really would be without a mother.

And then there was Katrina's sister to consider. How would she deal with the knowledge of what her sister had done? She was already grieving harder than I'd ever seen anyone grieve; would my sure-to-be popular article make her loss that much harder to deal with?

Rayleen, Trevor, Joshua, and Katrina were dead, and the gaping question in my mind was why? How had something as harmless as a simple argument turned into this huge black hole that had claimed so many lives?

I grabbed a blanket and a heavy sweater from my room, then went downstairs and poured myself a glass of wine. I took it out onto the deck, then settled into a lounge chair with the blanket tucked around me. I watched the waves roll in and out as I let the sound of the sea calm me. I had a decision to make, and in that moment it didn't feel like one I could make alone. I realized what I really needed was someone to talk things through with, so I called Jack and asked him to come over. Of all the people in my new life, for some reason I believed he would be the one who could best provide the insight I needed.

"That's quite some story," Jack said after I shared with him the story Brooke had told me. "What are you going to do?"

"For about two minutes I honestly thought I had a decision to make, but as I sat here reliving Brooke's story, I knew I only have one choice. I can't be responsible for sending her to jail. Not that she would necessarily end up there, but you never know how these things will work out. She *is* a good person with a good heart who got caught up in an impossible situation."

Jack put his arm around my shoulders and gave me a squeeze. "I know how much this article meant to you."

"It did, but there will be other opportunities to reclaim my life. Besides, I'm not sure the timing is right for me to return to New York, even if I was offered a job. I did promise Garrett I'd help with the remodel and I'd hate to let him down."

"You're an amazing woman, Jillian Hanford."

"Of course you realize you can't print the story either."

Jack shrugged.

"A story like that would have put your little paper on the map."

"I kind of like being off the map."

"I guess I should call Brooke to tell her what I've decided. I'm sure she's waiting on pins and needles to find out if I'm going to toss a live grenade into her life."

Jack rubbed his hand along my arm. "She made a wise choice in trusting you."

I didn't reply. I wondered why Brooke *had* decided to trust me. She didn't know me. I supposed she could see I was making progress in discovering what had happened and had no intention of giving up. Her plan to share what had occurred from her own perspective had provided an angle I might not have been aware of had I finally found the proof I needed on my own. Not that I would have, but she'd had no way of knowing how much progress I'd already made.

"What are you going to do about Savage?" Jack asked. "He's bound to figure things out sooner or later."

"I don't think he will. He seemed genuinely grieved when he thought Brooke might be the killer. If you and I let it go I think he'll let it fade away as well."

"Are you sure? He's a cop after all."

"I guess if he doesn't drop it we can just tell him what Brooke told me minus the part about her altering everyone's memory. But I doubt he'll pursue it. The only reason he started looking in to it in the first place was because I insisted on it."

Jack and I sat in silence, sipping our wine and listening to the sound of the sea. I pulled the blanket over both of us as the night grew colder and we relaxed into our own thoughts.

"Now that you're staying for a while," Jack whispered softly, "will you go out with me on a real date if I change my name?"

I couldn't help but laugh. "You'd seriously change your name just to go out with me?"

"If that was what it took."

"You know, you're crazy."

Jack winked. "Maybe, but I've been told I'm the best kind of crazy."

I rolled my eyes.

"So how about it? One date. We don't even have to tell anyone."

I looked into Jack's eyes. I could tell he was serious despite his light tone. "Okay. One date. If it works out we'll discuss the name change."

Jack smiled. "Deal."

Second Look published July 4, 2017

Five years ago award winning actor Rhett
Crawford threw a Halloween party for a group of
family members and friends. The party, which
actually took place over a four day weekend, was held
at his beachfront estate on Gull Island. On the third
night of the party the groundskeeper, Wylie Slater,
found the body of one of the guests, Georgia Darcy,
bludgeoned and left in the toolshed beyond the
garden. The authorities were notified immediately
and interviews of all guests on the property were
conducted. It was eventually determined that the
victim's date, a man named Dru Breland, had most
likely killed the woman before fleeing the scene of the
crime.

According to witness statements, Georgia and her date had been bickering constantly during the course of their stay, and more than one witness had seen Dru slap Georgia before stomping off on the night she died. The authorities conducted an exhaustive search but were unable to locate Mr. Breland. As far as anyone associated with the investigation could find out, he was never seen again. Dru was a wealthy man with a depth of resources. It was assumed by most that he had fled the country and started a new life elsewhere under an assumed name.

Then five days ago, the oceanfront estate, once owned by Rhett Crawford but now owned by an out of state developer, had been scheduled for demolition. During the destruction of the house a human skeleton was found in a hidden room off the wine cellar. After a thorough investigation by the medical examiner and his team, it was determined that the body in the hidden room was in fact the decomposed remains of murder suspect, Dru Breland. My friend Jackson Jones, owner of the fledging Gull Island News, latched onto the story and seems determined to find out who killed Georgia Darcy five years ago, and how her date, Dru Breland, ended up in the secret room.

Jack knew that the five year old mystery would be a complicated one to unravel, so he asked me, Jillian Hanford, if I would be willing to present the mystery to the writers group I currently lived and sleuthed with. I agreed to Jack's request which brings us to the regular Monday meeting of the eclectic group of writers I call friend but consider family.

Books by Kathi Daley

Come for the murder, stay for the romance.

Zoe Donovan Cozy Mystery:

Halloween Hijinks
The Trouble With Turkeys
Christmas Crazy
Cupid's Curse
Big Bunny Bump-off
Beach Blanket Barbie
Maui Madness
Derby Divas
Haunted Hamlet
Turkeys, Tuxes, and Tabbies
Christmas Cozy
Alaskan Alliance
Matrimony Meltdown
Soul Surrender
Heavenly Honeymoon
Hopscotch Homicide
Ghostly Graveyard
Santa Sleuth
Shamrock Shenanigans
Kitten Kaboodle
Costume Catastrophe
Candy Cane Caper

Holiday Hangover
Easter Escapade
Camp Carter – *July 2017*

Zimmerman Academy The New Normal

Ashton Falls Cozy Cookbook

Tj Jensen Paradise Lake Mysteries by Henery Press

Pumpkins in Paradise
Snowmen in Paradise
Bikinis in Paradise
Christmas in Paradise
Puppies in Paradise
Halloween in Paradise
Treasure in Paradise
Fireworks in Paradise – *October 2017*

Whales and Tails Cozy Mystery:
Romeow and Juliet
The Mad Catter
Grimm's Furry Tail
Much Ado About Felines
Legend of Tabby Hollow
Cat of Christmas Past
A Tale of Two Tabbies
The Great Catsby
Count Catula
The Cat of Christmas Present
A Winter's Tail
The Taming of the Tabby – *May 2017*

Seacliff High Mystery:
The Secret
The Curse
The Relic
The Conspiracy
The Grudge

Sand and Sea Hawaiian Mystery:
Murder at Dolphin Bay
Murder at Sunrise Beach
Murder at the Witching Hour
Murder at Christmas
Murder at Turtle Cove
Murder at Water's Edge – *June 2017*

Road to Christmas Romance:
Road to Christmas Past

Writers   Retreat   Southern Mystery:
First Case
Second Look – *July 2017*

Kathi Daley lives with her husband, kids, grandkids, and Bernese mountain dogs in beautiful Lake Tahoe. When she isn't writing, she likes to read (preferably at the beach or by the fire), cook (preferably something with chocolate or cheese), and garden (planting and planning, not weeding). She also enjoys spending time on the water when she's not hiking, biking, or snowshoeing the miles of desolate trails surrounding her home.

Kathi uses the mountain setting in which she lives, along with the animals (wild and domestic) that share her home, as inspiration for her cozy mysteries.

Kathi is a top 100 mystery writer for Amazon and she won the 2014 award for both Best Cozy Mystery Author and Best Cozy Mystery Series.

She currently writes five series: Zoe Donovan Cozy Mysteries, Whales and Tails Island Mysteries, Sand and Sea Hawaiian Mysteries, Tj Jensen Paradise Lake Mysteries, and Seacliff High Teen Mysteries.

Giveaway:

I do a giveaway for books, swag, and gift cards every week in my newsletter, *The Daley Weekly* **http://eepurl.com/NRPDf**

Other links to check out:
Kathi Daley Blog – publishes each Friday **http://kathidaleyblog.com**
Webpage – **www.kathidaley.com**
Facebook at Kathi Daley Books – **www.facebook.com/kathidaleybooks**
Kathi Daley Teen – **www.facebook.com/kathidaleyteen**
Kathi Daley Books Group Page – **https://www.facebook.com/groups/569 578823146850/**
E-mail – **kathidaley@kathidaley.com**
Goodreads – **https://www.goodreads.com/author/sho w/7278377.Kathi_Daley**
Twitter at Kathi Daley@kathidaley – **https://twitter.com/kathidaley**
Amazon Author Page – **https://www.amazon.com/author/kathi daley**
BookBub – **https://www.bookbub.com/authors/kat hi-daley**
Pinterest – **http://www.pinterest.com/kathidaley/**

Made in the USA
Lexington, KY
29 April 2017